A RETRO THRILLER

HALL OF MIRRORS

CHARLES ASHE

HEADSTONE BOOKS

Published by
HEADSTONE BOOKS
Delaware USA

First Edition
©2022 Charles Ashe
ISBN: 978-1-955741-14-9
Cat # HB001

Book design and formatting by Charles Ashe

www.charlesashe.com

For
Katie & Heidi

HALL OF MIRRORS

1

SCARECROW

A short, blood-curdling scream pierced the air above the cornstalks.

Danny spun around on the dirt path and sprinted in the opposite direction. He had lost Angela about five minutes ago and that scream sounded like her.

The tall stalks of corn towered on either side of him, guiding his frantic dash to the source of the scream. He jerked left, then right, then right again, and found himself at a dead end.

The twilight sky above the corn provided no landmarks, and Danny was losing his sense of direction. Should he turn around? The longer he hesitated, the more uncertain he was.

He shook his trembling hands, as if that would ease the creeping panic eating at his nerves.

No, he couldn't turn around. He'd get mixed up and not know which way to go.

Instead, he shut his eyes, drew in a breath, and threw himself into the thick wall of corn ahead. With a whoosh, he tumbled through onto a different path, wincing as he landed on his hands and knees.

Out of the corner of his eye, he saw a shadowy figure racing towards him—not Angela. Kicking up dust, he scrambled to his feet and ran.

As the path curved to the left, Danny lost his balance and stumbled over his own feet. He hurtled sideways and toppled into a small clearing among the cornstalks. He slammed into something solid and fell again.

Danny lifted his head enough to see he had crashed into a group of hay bales in the clearing. A wooden pole wobbled in the center of the bales. As he looked further up, he met the gaze of a scarecrow hung upon the pole, arms stretched out to the sides like a straw Jesus. The dirty sackcloth face, with angry, sunken black holes for eyes and thick black string stitched over the mouth, had a malevolent grimace. Its tattered denim overalls and purple flannel shirt flapped as it teetered.

Tommy had the same purple flannel shirt.

Fear flooded his chest when the grotesque figure creaked and moaned, then lurched at him. It struck his chest and knocked him to the ground, its dead weight pressing him against the dirt.

Danny screamed.

2

BAD APPLE

*A*ngela couldn't stop laughing.

"I'm glad I'm not the only one who was spooked by the scarecrow," she said, slapping her knee. "I wasn't paying attention and walked right into it. It's creepy as hell. The look on your face was priceless!"

"Is that why you screamed earlier? Well, you could have warned me instead of just waiting here in the dark!"

"But that would be no fun," Angela said.

Danny heaved the massive scarecrow upright, made sure it was steady, then slid the hay bales back in place around the base.

He had been having a lot of fun exploring Woodside Farm's eleven-acre corn maze, more fun than he'd allowed himself in a long time. Until he saw the scarecrow. Until he saw the purple flannel.

"Do you remember this shirt?" he asked. "Tommy had the same one."

The joy drained from his friend's face. "No."

"We had matching ones. Mine was orange and his was purple."

"Oh."

"My dad dumped a bunch of Tommy's clothes at Goodwill before he left town a few weeks ago. I wonder if this shirt was his... I suppose it could have ended up here."

"If I was going shopping for a scarecrow, I'd probably go to Goodwill before Macy's," Angela granted, "but it's probably not your brother's. There's more than one of those in the world."

"Yeah, I suppose so."

Although he admitted it was unlikely, he had to check the size. He climbed atop the hay bales and tugged the flannel collar down far enough to see the tag inside. Large. The same as Tommy's. Hmm.

A young girl wandered into the clearing with them, followed by her mother. Angela smiled at them. When Danny peered from behind the scarecrow, the youngster squealed with fright, then let out a peal of high-pitched laughter.

Angela motioned to a path leading out of the clearing. "I think that's the end of the maze there. Why don't we get out of here and have some apple cider and doughnuts?"

"Yeah, sounds like a plan."

As he and Angela crossed the field between the corn maze and the concessions shack, Danny drew a deep breath through his nose, filling his lungs with crisp September air. The aroma of sweet hay mingled with warm apples, cinnamon, and sugar.

Children and their parents sat at picnic tables surrounding the shack, eating sweets and sipping cider. Danny fought a tinge of jealousy. Such happy faces. Too happy. Couldn't at least one kid be throwing a tantrum or fighting with a sibling? The joy offended him, even though he'd been one of those cheerful people just moments earlier.

But that's how it was now. One small trigger changed his mood for days.

They stepped up to the line in front of the ordering window, the scent of delicious food wafting toward them.

He glanced at Angela, who peered back with worried eyes. Guilt mixed with Danny's sour mood. He was a downer, and he pulled Angela down with him.

"I'm sorry," he said. "But I warned you."

"I know. I know. It was worth a try, though, to do something fun."

Danny tensed up at the thought of talking about his problems near others in the concession line, so he changed the subject.

"So, what will you get?"

The limited menu of hot drinks and food swung on a hand-painted sign above the ordering window.

"I think the super spice cider and one cinnamon doughnut. It's crazy chilly for early September. I need some heat! What about you?" She pulled the sleeves of her floppy black sweater over her bangled wrists and hands.

"Ummm… Just a regular apple cider…and an apple sugar doughnut."

Danny and Angela had been close friends since fourth grade and were unaccustomed to awkward silences. Now one invaded their conversation, like an unwelcome stranger. After ordering, they carried their food to a table on the edge of the picnic area. The conversation they needed to have was looming, threatening them with every moment of silence.

Angela pressed her lips to the edge of her cup for a cautious sip of steaming cider. "Can I prefer summer over autumn and still be the badass goth chick of your dreams?"

7

A crooked smile formed on Danny's face. "Of course. Just don't listen to Morrissey. That's where I draw the line."

"Insufferable! No chance of that! What's your favorite season?"

Danny cupped his hands around his cider, letting the warmth permeate his skin. He surveyed the hills beyond the farm, where the tops of trees caught the last rays of the setting sun. The maples were already turning yellow and red.

"I'm definitely a fall guy."

This year, he'd hardly noticed the seasons, but today the unusually cool air triggered a melancholy within him. The last time it was cool outside, Tommy was alive. The last time it was cool outside, Tommy had died. A cloud of dread moved over him, as if history would repeat itself. Danny wondered if this was how grief worked, always threatening to circle back, like the seasons.

Another span of awkward silence.

"I know it's painful, Danny, but can we please talk about it now, just a bit?"

"I really don't know what to say."

"That's unlike you! Which is why I'm concerned. Not about today, I mean. More in a general sense. It's been seven months since…you left school, and I've only seen you three times. You've never once talked about Tommy. I mean, really talked about him. Am I a rotten friend? Do you not trust me?"

"Of course I trust you!" said Danny.

Angela wasn't a rotten friend, but she had a bad habit of trying to fix everyone's problems. She didn't understand that sometimes people needed to feel things, for better or worse. She was a great friend when life was good, but when things got complicated, she often overstepped, and could really grate.

Danny's mom had done her best to keep Angela at bay since March, filtering his phone calls and sending her away if she showed up on their doorstep. With the new school year starting, this tactic wasn't sustainable.

"I'm dealing with this the best way I can," continued Danny, "and mostly, that means avoiding people."

People could not only be insensitive but also inquisitive. Danny was afraid of both. It wasn't just Tommy's death that made life hard now; it was the circumstances of his death, and Danny couldn't bear anyone questioning him about it.

"Is it only people you are avoiding? Your mother says you've spent the past few months holed up in your room doing nothing but watching movies and taking naps. Maybe you need to see a grief counselor. My mom knows a therapist that specializes in grief. I could—"

"No. I'm not talking to a shrink."

It surprised him Angela didn't offer to do the counseling herself. She probably had enough gumption to believe she was an expert on death, since her father died when she was young. Losing a father at only five years old wasn't the same as losing Tommy.

Angela flipped her curly auburn hair away from her freckled face. "Are you ready to return to school tomorrow? You'll have to talk to people there."

"I'll be fine."

"I always imagined senior year would be the best year of high school. Off-campus lunches, driving to school, all the free periods, all the parties… It's dumb to have any expectations, ever, but…we can still make this a good year."

Danny felt the sting of her insinuations.

"Sorry to be such a disappointment. Maybe you should find a new best friend that meets all your expectations so you can salvage your senior dream."

"Don't you want a great senior year?"

Danny softened a bit. He, too, had always looked forward to the privileges of being a senior. "I'm really lost, Ange. It still hurts every day."

"I get it. I can't imagine losing a twin brother. But listen," she said, touching his hand, "I knew Tommy pretty well, and I don't think he'd want you to destroy yourself over him."

"Is that what I'm doing? Maybe it's what I deserve."

Angela blinked. "What? Why would you say that?"

"Look, I thought we came here for a distraction. Fun, right? Let's do the hayride now."

Danny decided he'd rather pretend to be happy than suffer this kind of interrogation. He stuffed the last bit of doughnut into his mouth and brushed the sugar off his fingers.

"Okay, I guess we can come back to this discussion later," said Angela.

"Or not."

They tossed their empty cups in the huge trash barrel beside the concessions shack and circled around it towards the hayride station.

Angela stopped suddenly, and Danny crashed into her. Ugh. He'd had enough of running into things and people and ideas today.

"What gives?"

She pointed at the side of the shack. "It's a poster for Woodside Farm's 1988 autumn carnival. Opens Sunday, October first. That's less than three weeks from now."

The corn maze and pumpkin patch were always the first to open at the farm, but the primary draw every year was the sprawling carnival that camped out for weeks in October. It had been years since Danny had any interest in going, even though his neighborhood was adjacent to the farm.

"We should go this year," said Angela, nudging him.

Danny hesitated, already formulating an excuse for not going, when something caught his eye. At the bottom right of the poster, after a row of other amusements, was a spooky picture of two hands hovering over a crystal ball with arcs of electricity between them.

The Magnificent MADAM MAGGIE, fortune teller— she knows your past and she sees your future—$10 for a reading

Danny's mind raced. He couldn't remember the carnival ever having a fortune-teller.

"Well?" Angela pressed him.

He wasn't the least bit interested in the carnival— too many people, too much noise. But this...*this* tempted him. Could Madam Maggie already know what he had done to Tommy? Could she tell him what he needed to know?

Eyes still locked on the poster, Danny mumbled, "Yeah. Totally. Let's go."

3
FIRST DAY OF SCHOOL

"*D*anny…sweetheart…it's time to get up. You have an appointment with Dr. Hughes before homeroom."

Danny flipped over in bed but didn't respond.

When Dad woke him and Tommy up in the morning, he didn't stand on the other side of the door and plead with them. He just came in and demanded, "Get out of bed." It was gruff but effective. Dad wasn't around anymore, though. Asshole.

His mom rapped lightly on his bedroom door again, then cracked it open.

"Danny…"

"Okay, I'm awake."

This had to be the most bizarre first day of school ever. He'd never had to do it alone before. He imagined himself going into school as an amputee, without a leg or an arm. That might be easier to explain than the truth.

Danny opened his eyes.

The early morning sun, reaching through his bedroom window, cast two orange squares of light on the opposite wall. That side of the room was empty, where Tommy's bed used to be.

A few weeks ago, in a fit of disgust over his grief, Danny had dismantled and removed Tommy's bed from the room. He had grown tired of waking up and looking over at the empty bed, thinking Tommy had woken up before him, only to remember the truth. Cursing, he had dragged the mattress and bed frame into the garage, determined to erase all memories of Tommy from their bedroom. Then he pulled all of Tommy's clothes out of his bureau and shoved them into a trash bag, took his cork board and his INXS poster off the wall, but then Danny stopped.

He didn't have the heart to take down Tommy's photography. So proud of his work, Tommy had carefully arranged his black and white photos in a grid on the wall above his bed. Mostly scenes around town and candid portraits of friends, the photos reflected Tommy more than his other belongings. They were images seen through his eyes and captured by his creative mind. The "good old days." Danny couldn't imagine life ever looking like that again. Everything was tainted.

Now, lost in a spiral of painful thoughts, Danny moaned and stuffed his face into his pillow. The guilt crept in again. The great void, the pain, was his doing. It was what he wanted, right?

Mrow.

Something soft bumped Danny's hand, which was slung over the side of the bed. Fur.

His orange tabby cat, Jonesy, rubbed his whiskered cheek on Danny's hand again.

Mrowwww.

"Ugh…you too, eh? Did mom send you in?"

Danny scratched Jonesy between the ears, making him purr.

"Alright, if you insist," Danny said and swung out of bed.

After showering and dressing, Danny sat in his Siouxsie & The Banshees T-shirt, eating a bowl of shredded wheat, eyes still only half open.

He was awake far too late the previous night and was paying for it now. Thoughts of Madam Maggie and the possibility of receiving a message from the other side filled him with anticipation. He had drawn in his sketchbook, recreating from memory the ad he saw the previous day. The hands, the crystal ball, the bolts of electricity representing the spark of knowledge he craved. It was 1:00 a.m. by the time he turned his lamp off and drifted into sleep, dreaming, fantasizing.

Madam Maggie knows the past and sees your future.

He cared little about the future. How could he when the past pulled him backward like an industrial-sized magnet? And what about the present? What about Tommy now? The poster said nothing about the present, but would Maggie still have something to say about it? Because the confusion was now, the pain was now.

Danny pulled his Mercury Lynx into the senior parking lot at school. He admitted it did feel kinda cool. The junior lot was so far away from the building.

As he walked into school, the few students already there at this early hour didn't seem to notice him at all.

Yet it was as if he had a big sign on his body, like a sandwich board you'd see in cartoons, slung over his shoulders. It advertised, in bright letters, "I'm the guy whose twin brother died last school year. Yes, I'm here alone!"

Danny made his way to the administration wing of the school and slipped into the guidance lobby.

Dr. Hughes adjusted her large horn-rimmed

glasses, then dipped her head down so she could peer over them at Danny. "So, how was your summer?"

"Really? What a shit question."

"No cursing, please."

"It was awful."

Danny shifted in the uncomfortable plastic chair and stared at the odds and ends scattered on Dr. Hughes' messy desk. A water bottle and a mug. A fake plant in a blue plastic pot. Some framed photos of a man and several children. Were they fake, too?

Danny didn't dislike Dr. Hughes personally, but he didn't see the point in this meeting. He had nothing to say to her, unless she wanted to talk about *Creepshow 2* or how *Spaceballs* was far superior to *Star Wars*.

"It looks like you successfully completed your night school courses over the summer. In fact, your grades are fantastic."

"Those classes are dumbed down."

"In any case, you had quite a lot to accomplish after missing so much time at the end of last year. Do you feel ready to take on your senior year?"

Danny thought of what Angela had said the day before about senior year. "No. I'm not excited about it. I wish I could stay in night school. It's quiet there."

"Well, I'm here to help make it easier in any way I can. Are you happy with your schedule?"

"It's fine."

"Is there anything about this year you are looking forward to?"

Danny stared at the ceiling. Was there an answer to that dumb question up there?

"Finishing high school, I guess."

"Have you thought about what you'd like to do after graduation?"

It was unnerving to think that he had any future at all.

Dr. Hughes opened a metal file drawer next to her desk and flipped through folders. "Sometimes when we experience trauma, like a tragic loss, we enter a survival state of mind and simply take one day at a time. Small accomplishments are good to recognize. Unfortunately, most of your peers are thinking about the big picture right now, about what's next, making important college decisions."

Just what Danny needed—another reason to feel alienated from everyone else at school. His peers were a disgustingly homogeneous sampling of humans, all the same age, in the same town, at the same high school, moving at the same speed, with the same boring aspirations. But Danny was different. If for no other reason because he carried an invisible parasite around with him. Among his peers, he cast the darkest shadow.

Dr. Hughes retrieved a thick, magazine-type book

with a few smiling, well-adjusted students on the front cover and flopped it down on the desk facing Danny.

"You missed the junior student interviews at the end of last year. When you're feeling up to it, look through this college applications guide. There's some information about specific colleges in the back, as well as trade schools. If you have questions about applying, come talk to me."

Danny was stunned, as if she had broken into a foreign language mid-sentence. Instead of speaking, he stared at the fake plant. So much dust. She should clean it.

"What is your greatest concern about this upcoming school year?" Dr. Hughes asked.

Danny looked up at the ceiling again. Greatest concern… Ah, yes.

"Having to pretend that I deserve a future, as if I didn't kill my brother."

4
KEVIN

*D*anny left Dr. Hughes' office and entered the small guidance lobby with an exit survey in hand.

"When you're finished, you can put the paper in the hanging bin on the outside of my office door," instructed Dr. Hughes.

"Okay."

He took a seat in a squarish chair, the kind that filled up every doctor's waiting room, and started filling out the form.

Thankfully, it was multiple choice and required little thought. He picked all the answers he thought they wanted to see.

"Hey, nice shirt!"

Danny looked up from the survey and his heart skipped a beat. One of the most beautiful faces he'd ever seen beamed at him from across the room—another student, sitting in a chair with the ankle of one leg propped on the knee of the other leg.

Shirt... Who has a nice shirt? Danny looked down at his Siouxsie Sioux T-shirt.

"Oh, thanks," Danny replied, realizing there was no one else present and the boy was talking to him.

Danny blushed as he looked back at the form on his lap. He tried to read the next question, but found it impossible to focus. He could feel sweat forming on his palms.

Who was that boy? He looked too old to be a freshman. But Danny had never seen him before.

"Have you heard *Peepshow* yet?"

Danny glanced back at the boy. That face, beaming, both boyish and manly at the same time. His eyes were bright and eager. Danny couldn't think clearly, so he looked aside as he replied, "The new Siouxsie album? Yeah. It's awesome."

"It's fantastic, actually."

"Yeah," Danny blurted, then stopped.

That's all? No, don't be dumb and awkward, he told himself.

"It's a different direction for them, but I'm digging

it," Danny added.

"Me too. I got it on tape, but you look like a CD guy. My buddy says CDs are going to take over and we won't be able to buy records or cassettes anymore."

The boy wore a faded, thinning black T-shirt that showed off his broad, round shoulders, and army green pants tucked into a pair of beat-up combat boots. His brown hair was short, with just a hint of a mohawk at the center. He looked like some kind of punk badass.

Danny's eyes stuck on the boy's thick bottom lip for a moment too long. Embarrassed, he looked back down at the survey he was supposed to be filling out, forgetting to say something about whether he bought tapes or CDs.

"Are you a new student?" the boy asked.

"No, just a broken one, I guess." Oh, God, *cringe*. What in the hell did that even mean? Danny was sure his face was bright red now.

"Oh, okay. Well, I'm new. Kinda sucks to transfer, but what can you do when your parents are lame enough to move before your senior year."

"Bummer," said Danny. "So...are you in the guidance office for orientation then?"

"Yeah. My appointment is soon. Also hoping to make a change to my schedule. Have you taken Mr. O'Quinn's US government class?"

"Ha! I'm taking it this semester, actually."

"No kidding! Hopefully we'll be classmates. I'm trying to get in. Do you know anything about O'Quinn?"

Hopefully we'll be classmates. That's what he said. Gah!

"I don't know much about him," admitted Danny. "Some people think he's an asshole. The way my schedule was planned, I didn't really have a choice but to take his class. I'm expecting it to be pretty boring. Government, ugh."

"Eh, I dunno. It's probably good to know how our government works. Or doesn't work."

He sounds smart, too. Beauty and brains.

"What about the rest of your schedule? What else are you taking?" asked Danny.

As the boy scratched his head and listed the other courses that made up his fall semester, Danny's heart sank.

"Ah, looks like we don't share any other classes."

The conversation flowed easily as it continued, so Danny's nerves calmed a bit. This guy was pretty easy to talk to, despite his intimidating good looks.

"My name is Kevin, by the way."

"Cool. I'm Danny."

For the first time in his life, he was ashamed of his name. In that moment, talking to Kevin, it sounded way too cute and juvenile coming out of his mouth. Maybe he should start going by "Dan"—that sounded more mature. Or maybe no matter what he said, he was going to be embarrassed. Kevin was so much cooler. *Ugh, whatever.*

Kevin hopped out of his seat and extended a hand.

"Nice to meet you, Danny. So you've got good taste in music. Who else do you listen to?"

Danny shook his hand, and Kevin backed into his seat again.

"Uhm, Sisters of Mercy, Depeche Mode, R.E.M., Bowie...I like a lot of different stuff. My friend Angela is the one who turned me on to goth stuff like Siouxsie."

"Bowie's cool. How about The Smiths?"

"No, sorry. Hard pass."

"Pet Shop Boys?"

"Uh, they're okay, I guess."

"Culture Club?"

He can't be serious.

Oh... Oh! He knows.

No one else knows.

Danny's nerves returned, pulled taut by the suggestion left hanging in the air. Kevin wasn't talking about music. Not really.

Luckily, Dr. Hughes reemerged from her office and broke the tension. "Kevin Pullman?"

He stood up. "Yep, that's me."

"Come on in and we'll get you sorted out," she said, heading back into her office.

"Hey Danny, maybe I'll see you in O'Quinn's class."

Kevin winked and disappeared into Dr. Hughes' office.

5

RUNNING WITH SHADOWS

"*I* know it's short notice," said Angela, "but I thought we could hang at my place, catch up, you know. My parents are gone for the weekend. I wanna hear about how your first week of school went."

Danny pinned the cordless phone between his ear and his shoulder and continued drawing little air bubbles floating out of puckered fish mouths. The two fish were unlike any he'd ever seen, and they were circling a scarecrow that was underwater.

"I talk to you every day in school. You already know everything about my first week back," he lied, thinking of Kevin.

The elusive Kevin.

Who hadn't shown up in his government class, but who crossed Danny's mind daily.

"Well," Angela persisted, "we can still reflect on your week. And there might be things I haven't told you about my week. C'mon, this is what friends do."

"Eh, I'm kinda busy with this drawing right now," he said. "Maybe we can talk on the phone while I work on it?"

"No. I want to see you. It's been ages since I painted your nails black, and I just got a new bottle of polish."

Danny sighed.

His first impulse was to remind her the last time she painted his nails black, his father had thrown a fit. No son of his would look like a devil worshipper, or worse! But his dad had moved across the country over a month ago, and his mom wouldn't admonish him for painted nails, so Danny couldn't use that excuse.

Resisting Angela was probably pointless, anyway. She would just become more annoying. Or angry.

"Fine. I'll be over soon."

Beep.

Danny pressed the power button on the phone before Angela could reply.

Danny leaned against the wall just outside the kitchen, watching his mother as she sat at the table, opening a pile of mail. She'd set the plastic trash can next to the table so she could toss empty envelopes and junk mail in as she worked her way through it all.

By most outward appearances, she was handling life much better than he was after the collapse of their family, but there were signs that wasn't the truth.

While she had always kept the house tidy, her preoccupation with cleaning had escalated to a neurotic degree. She was quick to snap at Danny for minor breaches of cleanliness, like a spot of toothpaste on the bathroom sink or forgetting to put the peanut butter away.

Ironically, she let a mountain of mail accumulate on the kitchen table—something she'd never allowed to happen before.

Danny knew she was a different person now that Tommy was gone, even though she tried not to show it.

"Mom?"

"Yes, sweetie?"

"Angela invited me over to hang out."

"That's very nice. Will you go?"

"Yeah. I won't be too late, though."

She looked up at him, one finger in a half-opened envelope, and smiled.

"It's okay, Danny. You're practically an adult now. And it's Saturday night. Go have fun."

Did she *want* him to leave? Danny couldn't tell.

He wanted to stay, wanted to draw in his sketch-book, only a room away from her, but he sensed that his withdrawal from life worried his mom. He didn't want her to worry anymore. So he'd go.

Danny turned to leave.

"Sweetie, could you take this trash out before you head out?"

"Sure."

Danny pulled the bag out and replaced it with a fresh one.

He swung the trash bag over his shoulder, like Santa's sack of toys, then crossed the kitchen to the back door.

Heading out, he called back, "Bye, Mom," and pulled the door closed behind him.

Danny saw it instantly.

A movement near the edge of the woods behind his house. Something out of place. Human-like. Dark.

At 8 p.m., the sky was a deep dark blue, on the cusp of night. Danny paused, straining to see across the half-acre of lawn separating the house and the woods.

He made one furtive step toward the trash bin at the back corner of the house and paused again, watching for any movement.

Only calm and quiet woods, so he walked over and heaved the bag inside the bin.

Probably nothing, he told himself.

Probably deer. Once in a blue moon, they'd come out of the woods and nibble the grass out in the open. He must have spooked it when he came outside, and it hopped into the trees.

But…

Maybe he'd take a walk over there and check it out before heading to Angela's house. The shape hadn't really struck him as a deer.

Danny was halfway across the backyard when it moved again. *There!* About ten feet deep into the woods. A dark figure dashed off, cracking sticks and tearing the underbrush as it went.

A surge of terror struck Danny. He spun on his heels and ran back to the house. He grabbed the knob on the door, twisted.

Locked. Of course.

He fumbled with his jacket pocket and his house keys flew out, fell at his feet.

Shit.

The unknown danger behind him crawled up his back like an electric eel.

Danny scooped up the keys and swiftly unlocked the door, rushed in, and slammed it shut.

"What is— Danny, what's wrong?"

Panting, he opened his mouth, but nothing came out.

He couldn't tell her. Anyone else in the world could say they'd seen a dark figure in the woods, but not Danny. It would be insane for him to suggest. In fact, it would be best to not even acknowledge those woods existed.

"Uhm, I…"

He dared a peek through the glass on the door. Nothing out there.

"I, uh, just felt very ill suddenly."

"Aww, hope you aren't coming down with something. Angela will understand. Give her a call."

If he didn't go, Angela would be annoyed.

Who the hell was that? And why were they behind his house?

He couldn't leave now.

As his mother tossed the last of the junk mail in the trash can and moved it back in place, Danny picked up the harvest gold telephone on the kitchen wall and dialed Angela's number.

"Goodnight, sweetie, I'm heading to my room now."

Danny smiled and nodded.

The telephone buzzed in his ear as he waited for Angela to pick up. He waited. And waited. No one answered. He finally hung the phone back on the receiver and retreated to his own bedroom.

The scarecrow and the fish beckoned him from the open sketchbook at his desk. He picked up his 3B pencil…then put it back down.

Ugh. Why didn't Angela answer her phone? Before he could relax, he'd have to let her know he wasn't coming.

He let a minute pass, then tried calling again on his cordless phone. Still no answer.

Maybe she wasn't answering because she didn't want to give him an opportunity to cancel. She was clever like that. And yet she'd still get pissy if he didn't show up.

Danny would have to go.

Before leaving, he peered out his window, which overlooked the backyard and the woods. No shadowy figure. But that didn't mean it wasn't somewhere out there, ready for…whatever.

Danny left through the front door this time, eyes darting in all directions as he headed down the sidewalk toward Angela's house.

Only three blocks and he'd be safe. They were big suburban blocks. But only three.

He sprinted over the first cross street. One block down.

At the halfway mark between their houses, he noticed it. A black shape near the curb, directly in front of Angela's house.

Danny's heart pounded. He darted behind a car parked on the street nearby. How did it know where he was going? Was it a monster intent on killing everyone he cared about? He held as still as he could bear and tried to breathe softly.

Laughing.

Someone was laughing and talking.

Danny slid just far enough beyond the car to steal a glimpse at the dark shape. It moved, revealing another dark shape on the other side of it.

Two people. Dressed in black. One with lighter hair. It was difficult to tell in the darkening dusk, but Danny thought it might be ginger hair. And then it all came together. Angela was sitting on the curb with someone else.

Relieved but also kinda embarrassed, Danny slunk out of his crouching position behind the car.

"Danny…?"

Damnit, she saw him.

"What are you doing sitting on the curb like that?" he asked.

"What are you doing hiding behind a car?"

As he approached, Danny identified the other person as Claudia, a senior at Woodside High and the only other goth kid they knew at school. Claudia and Angela had forged a friendship in sophomore year over their mutual love of all things dark and unusual.

Despite sharing four years of art classes with her, Danny was never sure if Claudia was truly his friend, too. His relationship with her was only by default, a tenuous extension of her friendship with Angela, even though he'd met her first.

"Good evening, Daniel," said Claudia, flicking ash from a clove cigarette.

"Hi Claudia. What are you guys up to?"

"Just waiting for you to arrive. Nancy's on her way, too."

Danny's face burned with irritation. Angela didn't mention other people would be there, and he wasn't up for a party. Maybe this could be his excuse for not staying.

He should have guessed Nancy would be coming when he saw Claudia. The two girls were stuck together like glue, inside and outside school, even though they formed an odd pair. Claudia's dour, above-it-all, world-weary attitude contrasted with Nancy's bubbly charm. Maybe Claudia needed someone to latch on to since her boyfriend graduated last year and moved away for college. But why Nancy?

"Have a seat, Daniel-san," said Angela, patting the curb next to her.

Layered under Danny's irritation with Angela was the lingering anxiety of being outdoors, vulnerable to that dark figure that was no doubt still lurking somewhere.

"Actually, can we go inside? It's getting chilly out

here."

Claudia lifted an incredulous eyebrow. "I'm going to finish my cigarette and wait for Nancy."

"Uhh, well, we told Nancy we'd be outside waiting for her. She's never been here before. Why don't I get you a jacket from inside?" Angela suggested. "I'll be right back!"

Danny followed her toward the house. "I'll come with you."

Once inside, Danny said, "I'm not staying."

"Ugh. Don't be like this."

"You didn't tell me Claudia and Nancy would be here."

"You wouldn't have come if I did. But you're here now, so let's just relax and have some fun."

Angela turned and opened the hall closet.

"I don't need a jacket. I just came to say that I'm not feeling so—"

Angela stopped and cocked her head, waiting for the excuse that she would not believe.

And then it tumbled out of Danny.

"There was something in the woods."

Angela's face tightened. "What?"

"I can't stay…because…there's something in the woods, and I…"

His mother was home alone with that thing out there somewhere.

"I can't leave my mom alone. There was some-thing…a person, stalking our house. I need to go back and make sure my mom is okay."

"There was nothing in the woods," Angela said.

"How do you know?"

"Because you don't want to hang out, that's how I know. You just want to go home and draw and watch movies and not spend time with me. With your friends."

"You don't believe me?"

Angela slammed the coat closet shut.

"Go, Danny. Just go."

Danny stood there, conflicted. He didn't want her to be angry, but he also didn't want to stay. Tommy never would have made such a mess of things.

Angela sighed.

"I'm not mad. See you in school on Monday, okay?"

"Okay."

A car door slammed outside.

"I'm sorry, Ange."

Danny twisted one hand nervously in the other.

"I know."

The front door whooshed open, and Claudia entered, with Nancy right behind, in pink sunglasses. *Why is she wearing sunglasses at night?*

"Hi Angela! Oh, hi Danny!"

"Hi Nancy."

"Oh yeah, hey," said Nancy. "It's good to see you, Danny, like, even if your brother isn't here. He was a good acquaintance, but he's better off now."

What? What the hell does that even mean? Danny was speechless.

"I think," Claudia said, "she means he's in a better place."

"I...okay. I'm going."

Danny slid past them and left.

6
GOVERNMENT

"Angela!" Danny called to her as he made his way through the noisy, crowded halls of Woodside High School.

Built in the 1920s, Woodside High School's historic interior of plaster walls and dark wood moulding created a mood inside that Danny thought was cool. But there were trade-offs, like lots of stairs spanning its three stories and very narrow hallways. Moving between classes sometimes felt like wriggling around in a can of sardines. It was a wonder that anyone made it to their next class on time.

Angela craned her neck around and her eyes

brightened. Although she and Danny hadn't discussed the incident at her house over a week ago, they had both moved on.

"Hey Daniel-san. How's it hanging?"

A space opened in the crowd, and Danny darted through, catching up to her. "Not too bad. On my way to O'Quinn's government class."

"I heard he's in a mood this year. He's been running his classes like a deranged drill sergeant. Tread carefully."

"That sounds about right. He's a bully."

"Let me know if he says anything weird to you. I have no problem giving him a piece of my mind."

Angela looked fantastic again, with her chin-length auburn hair teased out, partly concealing a pair of long, dangling earrings, her flouncy black blouse contrasting nicely with her tight black jeans, and her heavy black eyeliner painted in a cat-eye style. Even on a bad day, Danny's pride soared when he walked through school with her. She made him look good.

"So, the carnival opens on Saturday," Danny said. "Are we still going?"

"Yeah! How about I pick you up at seven?"

"Awesome. I'll be ready."

"Okay! I've gotta run to trig class now. Wish me luck!"

Angela turned to leave when a tall guy in a varsity

jacket knocked into her shoulder and continued down the hall.

"Hey, watch it, bozo!" she scolded.

"Oh, I will. I got my eyes on you, Count Chocula!" he said over his shoulder.

Angela giggled. "Don't look worried, Danny. That's just how Brock and I flirt."

"Ew, gross."

Danny paused at the open door of room 306. He made a silent wish, then entered.

Two weeks had passed with no sign of Kevin in Mr. O'Quinn's US Government class. Danny had spotted him in the halls a few times. His heart would jump into his throat and his mind would blank, thinking only of that beautiful face. He was beginning to fear that maybe Kevin hadn't been able to secure a spot in the class, that the opportunity to know him better had slipped away.

But today, he showed up.

Kevin waltzed through the door, spotted Danny immediately, and slid into the desk next to him.

"Hey Danny."

Oh God, he remembers my name.

"What's up, Kevin? Looks like you made it into O'Quinn's class."

"Glad to get my schedule sorted finally. Hughes

wouldn't let me in. She said the class was full. But someone dropped it, so here I am."

"Great. Welcome."

Kevin withdrew a black and white composition notebook from his bookbag and opened to a blank page. "So what did I miss?"

"Uh, well… The first week was just a syllabus review. Then we started the first chapter in the textbook, about the colonial period. We have a quiz scheduled next week."

"I don't have a textbook yet. I think I'm supposed to get one from the school store."

"Ah, the store's outside the gym. If you don't know where that is, I'd be happy to show you."

"That'd be great, Danny. Thanks."

Mr. O'Quinn strolled into the room with his typical tough-guy gait, like a corrections officer in a prison. Middle-aged, with gray, thinning hair, and a potbelly on an otherwise square, fit frame, he projected an air of masculine authority—one which no doubt brimmed with insecurities.

He surveyed the room, as if looking for opportunities to assert himself.

During the first day of class this year, he spent more time talking about the students than government. Most atrociously, he insinuated that a girl wearing a crop top was just asking to be assaulted by "libidinous males."

When lecturing on class material, he made no attempt to be neutral in his explanation of government and politics. He often digressed to air personal grievances or criticize the younger generation for being lazy and weak.

What Angela had heard about him was right, and that made Danny nervous. If it wasn't for the hope of Kevin joining the class, he may have dropped it.

Danny wondered how Kevin would react to Mr. O'Quinn.

"So...someone with a feeble mind has already dropped out of my US Government class. And just as quickly, we have a new recruit..." With his eyebrows high in his forehead, straining to see, the teacher looked at the new student sheet in his hand. "Mr. Kevin Pullman...?"

Kevin raised his hand. "Yes, sir, right here."

"Pullman, what is that on your head? Are you some kind of communist?"

"Sir...?"

"Your hair. Or what's left of it."

"I'm growing a mohawk, sir."

Kevin's deferential tone surprised Danny.

"Well, we'll see about that," Mr. O'Quinn grumbled.

Kevin's face reddened and his hands balled into white-knuckled fists, like he was ready for war. *Okay, so maybe he recognizes Mr. O'Quinn for what he is. Didn't take long.*

Some students darted into the room a few seconds before the bell and took a seat. Mr. O'Quinn closed the door, then picked up a stick of chalk to write the day's notes on the blackboard while the class chatted quietly.

Kevin closed his eyes and took a deep breath through his nose. That seemed to do the trick.

"Do you think I could borrow your notes tonight?" he asked. "I suppose I should try to catch up in this class before Mr. O'Quinn targets me again."

Danny hesitated. He certainly would like to do anything to gain favor with Kevin but handing over his notebook to a complete stranger was too much. He had little drawings and other embarrassing things in there.

"Uhm, maybe I could write out a copy of the notes for you after school? It's just that I have notes for other classes in this book. And I need them. Tonight."

"I guess that would be okay. Or maybe instead we could study together after school? There is that quiz coming up next week, too."

Study together? *Oh God.*

"Okay, that would be great. Good. I mean, yeah."

Stay cool, Danny.

"It'd be nice to have a friend I can study with. You

know, being new here and all," said Kevin.

"Sure, of course."

"We could even do it at your place."

Danny nearly fell out of his chair at the thought of Kevin in his house, in his bedroom. But his mother would ask too many questions.

"Yeah, or your house," said Danny.

Kevin's mouth twisted. "Oh, well, uh, that might not be good. See, I'm living out of a hotel room with my parents right now. They're still trying to find a new house in Woodside."

"Alright, well, my house it is, then."

"Is Saturday night good?"

"Oh, my friend Angela and I are going to the Woodside Farm's carnival that night. How about Sunday?"

"It's a date," Kevin said, winking a hazel eye at him again.

Whoa.

Danny cracked a smile and then looked away, overcome with shyness.

7

CARNIVAL

While waiting for Angela to arrive, Danny sat in an armchair near the bay window at the front of his house and flipped through his sketchbook. Next to several drawings of the hands and crystal ball, he'd scribbled some questions and thoughts to prepare for his reading with the fortune-teller.

For the first time in a long time, he sensed things were falling into place. He had something to look forward to that excited him. He was hopeful. He was ready.

Danny shot up at the sight of Angela coming up the driveway. He grabbed his car keys from the hook near the kitchen phone.

"Ange is here, Mom! I'm leaving for the carnival!"

"Okay, sweetie, have fun! And say hello to Angela for me!"

Woodside Farm's paved lot was full, so Danny parked his car in the grassy lot beyond it.

He and Angela paid the four-dollar fee and entered. The smell of funnel cake and cotton candy, the whooshing sounds of rides whipping around and organ music from the carousel, the flashing yellow, red, and green in a cacophony of sparkling lights—all of it invigorated and exhausted Danny's senses.

Angela surveyed the scene. "What should we do first?"

"I guess we need to get tickets."

Danny never told Angela his true motive for going to the carnival. He planned, through gentle coaxing, to guide them along a path to the fortune-teller's tent.

Danny couldn't see Maggie's tent from where they were. The amusements were thick and deep, filling what seemed like ten acres of space sprawled out before them. With three hours left until the carnival closed for the night, he was sure they'd find it in time. Nevertheless, Danny fought his impatience. He wanted to find Madame Maggie as soon as possible.

Standing in line at the ticket booth, Danny said,

"Why don't we hit the Ferris wheel next? That way we can get the lay of the land from up high?"

"Great idea!"

After purchasing a strip of twenty tickets each, they headed toward the Ferris wheel, but Claudia and Nancy intercepted them.

"Oh my God," screamed Nancy, "I didn't know you guys would be here tonight!"

Danny tensed. Why did he feel so repulsed by Nancy? She meant well, he supposed.

"Hey! Hey!" said Angela. "Did you just get here? Anyone else from school here?"

"Billy Newsome and Jessica Handler are here somewhere," said Claudia. "Amy Metzinger is working the pony rides. I think her family owns the animals. Oh, and that new kid is wandering around by himself."

Kevin? Danny wasn't sure what to think about that. He was on a mission and needed to focus on his plan. Oh, what a distraction Kevin would be.

"What have you chicks done so far?" asked Angela.

Nancy held up a small stuffed panda with pink-and-white fur. "I won this at a balloon darts game! And we went on the Zipper, the Gravitron, the Tilt-A-Whirl, the Ferris wheel—"

"Actually," Danny interjected, "we were just headed to the Ferris wheel."

"Oh," Nancy sighed. "Maybe we can do some rides

together later. Enjoy the view. Don't fall off! Hahaha!"

The view from atop the Ferris wheel was impressive. Danny could see all of Woodside Farm, including the orchards, the corn maze, and pumpkin patch, and the far reaches of the carnival setup. Beyond that was the interstate highway tucked into the hills, and even further, the glow of downtown.

Danny spotted a purple tent on the border of the carnival, where it pushed up against the adjacent woods. Aside from the large white concessions canopy, it was the only tent. It had to be Madame Maggie. He made a mental note of the location.

The wheel paused for ten seconds or so at every quarter turn. When their car reached the peak and stopped, high above the din of fun and games, Danny allowed a calm to overcome him. He closed his eyes for a moment and focused on the atmosphere up here. A slight breeze rippled his hair. He imagined he was a bird ascending higher and higher in the twilight sky.

When Danny permitted himself to relax, he could be quite romantic. "Oh Angela, look at that sunset. So beautiful."

"Yeah," Angela said, but she seemed more captivated by the jumble of people and lights below. "Oh, I see Billy and Jessica!"

Danny picked out the midpoint between the Ferris wheel and Madam Maggie's tent. Right about there was the Round Up, an open-air version of the Gravitron that spun on a forty-five-degree tilt. Then he picked the midpoint between the Round Up and Madam Maggie's tent: the Scrambler. So, in order, the Round Up, then the Scrambler, then they'd be within view of the tent.

"Let's hit the Round Up next," Danny said. "I love that one!"

"Okay," Angela agreed. "But let's see if there are any cool games to play along the way. Maybe one with a black stuffed animal prize."

Angela grinned through black lipstick.

"Okay, sure. Yeah."

After playing both ring toss and water guns with no winner between them, they enjoyed a comical ride on the Round Up with a wailing, cursing grandmother who launched into a sneezing fit midway through.

Danny made a bid for the Scrambler next, which would put them within view of the fortune-teller's tent. Angela seemed happy to go with the flow this time and kept her eyes peeled for black game prizes on the walk over.

As they approached the line for the Scrambler, Claudia and Nancy appeared again. This time Claudia looked annoyed; Nancy was stumbling around and slurring her speech. She dropped her stuffed panda and almost toppled over while trying to pick it up.

"I leave her alone for two minutes, and this is what happens! She said some guy gave her a drink. I assumed it was soda or something and I let her drink it. She's sloshed now."

"Oooahlsh!" Nancy blubbered. "Let's ride a Scramlener!"

"I don't think spinning rides are a great idea in your state," said Claudia. "In fact, you're probably done with rides tonight. You're gonna lose your dinner."

Danny saw an opportunity. "Look, there's the Hall of Mirrors! I bet that'd be hilarious when you're wasted."

The Hall of Mirrors was next to Madam Maggie's tent.

Angela laughed. "Oh, the Hall of Mirrors is a tough maze. I did it last year. Let's put Nancy in there. Haha!"

"Yesshh," agreed Nancy.

Claudia rolled her eyes. "Okay, but then we're leaving."

As the group rushed off to see how the drunken Nancy would fare in a battle against hundreds of mirrors, Danny pulled Angela back.

"Hey, I'm going to get a reading from the fortune-teller next door," he said.

"Do you want me to go with you?"

"No. I want to do this alone."

"Okay, Daniel-san. We'll meet you out here when we're all done."

8

MADAM MAGGIE

*M*adam Maggie's tent was just as glorious as Danny had imagined it would be. The square structure radiated mystery, with thick purple fabric draped on all sides, and a peaked top adorned with gold suns and silver moons. The entrance flap was designated by a much lighter shade of fabric and heavy gold fringe bordered the top. To the left of the entrance stood a wooden sign with the familiar image of two hands hovering over a crystal ball, and "Madame Maggie, Fortune Teller" painted above it in large letters.

There was no one outside the tent and no line to get in. Did no one else care to know their future? Maybe

Tommy cleared a path for him. Or maybe it was just meant to be. That thought sent chills through him.

Danny stepped up to the stanchion at the entrance, unsure of what to do. The unmistakable scent of incense emanated from within.

"Hello?" he called out.

"Just a minute!" croaked a voice inside.

Shuffling, whispering.

A moment later, the entrance flap shifted, and a woman emerged. She was not at all what he expected her to be. She couldn't have been over thirty and was dressed like an average person plucked off the street.

"Hi, there's something important I need to talk about, and I need you to help because it's really bothering me and it's kind of important. My brother—"

"She's inside, kid. Excuse me."

The woman unhooked the stanchion, and a small group of children skipped over to her. She wasn't Maggie, she was a customer.

Danny's face reddened with embarrassment. Not only had he mumbled a bunch of nonsense to a stranger, but he had addressed the wrong person. Not a good start.

"Yes, hello…? Come in."

Danny took a deep breath to clear his head, pulled the entrance flap aside, and stepped in.

Madam Maggie sat behind a small round table in

the center of the room, with a crystal ball in front of her. She was at least twenty years older than the other woman and looked more like a fortune-teller should, with her wizened face and layers of gold bracelets, rings, and hooped earrings. Her frizzy black hair exploded sideways from underneath her headwrap.

Two candelabras on the floor illuminated the space on either side of the tent, and a dimly lit electric chandelier hung over the table. The fabric making up the walls must have been thick, as the cacophony of the carnival was muted inside.

"Ten dollars for a reading."

Danny fished a ten-dollar bill out of his pocket and placed it on the table.

"Have a seat," she said.

Danny sat himself on the wobbly wooden stool opposite Maggie. Her smile was kind and put him at ease.

"What is your name, my child?"

"Danny."

"And when is your birthda—" She stopped fussing with her headscarf and studied him for a moment. "Danny, eh? That's right. I've been expecting you, Danny. Danny Douglass."

He gasped. "You have?"

"Yes, you've come to me about something very important. I know you have a burning desire within you, Danny. But there's something standing in your way, and you need my help. Isn't that right?"

"Yes, that's exactly right."

"Mmhmm. Let us see what we can do about that."

Madame Maggie waved her hands over the crystal ball and looked deep inside, as if her eyes focused on something miles away. The poster illustration had come to life. Danny's heart raced with excitement.

"You have been feeling hopeless lately. Many people around you don't know the truth about you. Worst of all, you have been doubting yourself."

Danny's eyes welled up with tears. It was true, and for the first time since Tommy left, Danny felt understood, no longer alone in the world.

"Yes. My brother died. March of this year. I'm so confused. How did you know I was coming to see you?"

Maggie grunted. "Your desire is…let's see…is for a return to normal. You crave the comfort and security you once had. Isn't it so?"

"Yes. It's hard to find solid ground when…someone you've known since you were born—your twin—is suddenly just, gone. How can I—"

"Wait! There is more… Your doubts are about your brother's death. They are about your involvement in his death. Oh! I see…evil."

Maggie drew back in her carved wood chair,

shifting her gaze from the crystal ball to Danny. Her eyes, they had fear in them.

"You have a darkness in you, Danny. Sometimes it feels like someone else takes control of you, doesn't it?"

Danny trembled, shaking a tear loose from his eye.

"You feel as if you've crossed the threshold into wickedness and you can never go back."

"Please, Madam Maggie," Danny sobbed. "I need an answer to one question. Just one question, please."

"What is it, my child?"

"Does Tommy forgive me?" Danny covered his face with his hands, as if defending himself from the answer.

"I can't tell you what the dead think, dear—that would require opening a line of communication with the spirit world. A séance."

"Okay, yes," Danny agreed.

"I cannot perform a séance here, now. I must stay open for other customers." Maggie's chair creaked as she leaned toward him. "And it is much more expensive than a standard reading."

"Fine. I'll get the money. When can you do it?"

"I'm sorry, dear child. I am here every night until the carnival leaves town."

"It closes every night at eleven. Can you find some time after it closes? Please, Madam Maggie. I don't know anyone else that can perform a séance. Please!"

She paused for a moment. Some chatter grew louder at the entrance of the tent. There were others waiting to see her.

"Gah! My assistant quit just before the carnival opened here in Woodside. I am not used to doing this all on my own."

"Hellooo?" someone called.

"Wait your turn!" she barked.

Maggie turned her attention back to Danny. "Two weeks from today. Eleven p.m. Bring some friends to form a spirit circle. And it'll be a hundred dollars."

Danny stood up to leave. "Thank you, thank you."

"Oh, and Danny—there is one last thing…"

"Yeah?"

"The most important thing you need to know… This darkness within you is in danger of taking over, replacing you. If you cannot control it, more people will die."

9
NEGATIVE NANCY

*D*anny paced in the empty space between the tent and the Hall of Mirrors, waiting for the girls to emerge. Crowds of people passed in front of him, but Danny didn't notice them; his thoughts consumed him.

You have a darkness in you, Danny...

The words reverberated in his mind. If it was true, how did this darkness get there, inside him? Was he born with it, or did he invite it in somehow?

It may be better to focus on the positive. The most fantastic thing, that he hadn't even expected to come from his meeting with a fortune-teller, was that he'd be able to talk to Tommy again. In two weeks.

But what if Tommy was angry with him…?

You have a darkness in you, Danny…

A few kids exited the Hall of Mirrors with odd looks on their faces. Danny couldn't interpret the meaning, but it didn't look good.

First one, then another, then a series of shouts broke out from within the maze. Danny eyed the ticket taker at the entrance, who hopped off his stool, closed the gate, and rushed inside. Danny took a position nearer the exit, on the opposite end, and listened.

Then it registered. The shouts inside were calling out for Nancy.

"Nancy, Nancy!"

Danny darted into the exit. He didn't make it very far before crashing into Angela, who was barreling out in the opposite direction.

"Danny! How long have you been out here? Did you see Nancy come out?"

"No. I mean, I don't think so. Why? What's wrong?"

"We lost her! She's gone. She was between me and Claudia, but then disappeared before we were even halfway through. Claudia and I finished the maze and then backtracked and she's nowhere. She vanished!"

Claudia and the ticket taker searched the Hall of Mirrors once more, with no luck.

A long line of people had formed at the entrance, some curious about the halt in ticketing, and others growing impatient over the standstill.

"Where could she have gone?" Claudia asked. "Damnit. *Damnit*."

Claudia's distress was pronounced, suspiciously excessive.

"Why don't we split up and search the rest of the carnival?" said Angela. "Maybe she came out before us and is wandering around."

"Okay," Claudia agreed. "Let's meet back here in twenty minutes."

Danny tried to remember what Nancy was wearing as he snaked through the crowd. A light pink jacket, acid wash jeans, and her sunglasses with the pink lenses.

Danny rushed up to a girl that fit the description, ready to grab her shoulder and whirl her around, when she turned and he realized it wasn't Nancy.

As time elapsed, the crowds thinned, making it easier to search, but also more hopeless—there was no sign of her anywhere.

The three friends regrouped near the Hall of Mirrors at the appointed time.

Unsure what to do next, they milled about until finally accepting there was nothing else to be done.

Claudia left without her friend, promising to visit

Nancy's parents straight away to break the news of her disappearance. Maybe she found a way home.

Angela dropped Danny off at his house.

As he lay in bed, drifting into sleep, he remembered his reading with Madam Maggie.

You have a darkness in you, Danny...

Danny called Angela before breakfast the next morning, eager to know if there had been any developments overnight. He fidgeted, slipping his finger inside the coiled kitchen telephone cord while waiting for her to pick up the phone.

"Danny," she said, "the police were at my house this morning."

"What?!"

"They found Nancy. She was in the woods behind the Hall of Mirrors. She's in a coma!"

"Oh my God, what happened to her?"

"I suppose they don't know yet, and that's why the police questioned me. She has severe head trauma."

"What?! That's awful!"

"The police will probably get in touch with you, too. I told them you were there. Call me if they come to you. Actually, wanna hang tonight?"

"Uh, well, I would, but I can't. I'm studying with a friend later."

"A friend? What friend?"

"Someone from my US Government class. He's a new student and missed some things, so I agreed to help him catch up before a quiz."

The doorbell rang, followed by a hard, assertive knock.

"Angela, I think the police are here. I haven't told my mom yet about Nancy. I gotta go."

After letting the officer inside, they sat in the living room with his mother, who wore an apron over her morning robe and held a spatula, looking like a gobsmacked hausfrau as Danny spoke.

"I was at the carnival from about seven o'clock until right before it closed."

"Sir, what is this about?" asked his mom. "Danny, what happened?"

"Nancy went missing last night," he explained. "I would have told you, but you were already in bed when I got home."

Her mouth opened and she put a hand on her cheek. "Oh…no."

"So you didn't see Nancy come through the exit while you were waiting there?" the officer asked.

"No. I mean, I might have missed her, but I don't know. Maybe she came out before I left Madam Maggie's tent?"

Danny recalled how distracted by his own thoughts he had been. He supposed it was possible that she came out, and he just didn't notice.

"How well do you know Nancy?"

"She's more Claudia and Angela's friend than mine. We've had some classes together, but she's more of an acquaintance. A friend of a friend."

"No romantic involvement?" the officer pushed.

Danny blushed. "No."

"Do you know anyone that might have wanted to hurt her?"

"No. I don't know her well enough to say."

"Claudia? Angela?"

"No, no."

"Did she upset anyone at the carnival? Maybe she said something rude to staff or something along those lines?"

Danny wasn't with her long enough to witness anything like that. But he did see her drunk. Someone who worked there gave her a drink.

"Well, there was…"

Danny stopped himself. He knew she was drunk, and he suggested they go into the Hall of Mirrors. That triggered a pang of guilt. Maybe he'd keep that bit of information to himself.

"No, I can't think of anything like that," he answered.

Then it occurred to him he could be a suspect. How much did this man know about him already? Did he know his brother had died?

"Sir," Danny probed, "are you certain this was an assault? Could it have been an accident?"

"Assault?" gasped Danny's mother. "I thought she went missing. Now she's been assaulted, too?"

"It's too early to make any determination. We're trying to gather the facts right now."

"Right. Okay, thanks."

The officer stood up.

"If you remember anything else about last night that might help, call us."

Danny's mother escorted the officer out, then returned to mixing pancake batter, a flood of questions pouring out of her. Before Danny could answer any of them, the doorbell rang.

It was the officer again. "Does that car parked on the street belong to someone here?"

"Yes, it's my car," said Danny.

"Do you know your front passenger door isn't closed?"

"Oh…no."

"If the door was open all night, check if anything's missing, like your registration. And check your battery, too. The interior light is on."

Danny, still in his pajamas, followed the officer outside. As he approached his car, he saw something sitting on the passenger seat that made his heart sink.

How could it be?

Sitting upright on the seat was a small pink-and-white stuffed animal. Nancy's panda bear.

10
STUDYING

"That's kinda crazy, isn't it?" Kevin said, as he poked around Danny's bedroom, inspecting pictures on the walls, picking up this and that.

"Yeah. I feel just awful about it. I wonder if the guy who served her alcohol will be in trouble?"

"Maybe, if they know who it was."

Danny hesitated, on the brink of telling him about the pink panda, but he hadn't even told Angela yet.

After spotting the panda in his car, he'd searched the glove box like the officer suggested. There was nothing missing. Then he waited until the police officer got in his cruiser and left before he grabbed the stuffed animal and went inside. He concealed the fuzzy thing under his shirt so his mother wouldn't see. Now it lurked in his closet, like a monster.

Was it some kind of sick joke?

Could Angela have left it in his car last night? But she didn't have it with her earlier when they were searching for Nancy.

Did the cop see it? Did he plant it there?

Or was the truth more disturbing? Could it have been Danny himself that put it there?

You have a darkness in you, Danny... More people will die...

Kevin punched the power button on Danny's stereo. He had a Gene Loves Jezebel record in his hand. "I see I was partly right. You've got both CDs *and* vinyl. Should we put some music on?"

"I'm not sure I can study with music on."

"Oh, right."

Kevin tapped the button again to turn the stereo off and slipped the record back in the crate on the floor.

Danny heard Jonesy pawing at the door, so he let him inside. The cat padded his way over to Kevin and rubbed his head against Kevin's leg.

"Cute cat."

"That's Jonesy. He's very friendly."

"Okay," said Kevin, uninterested.

Frustrated, Jonesy sauntered away and pawed at the

closed bedroom door again.

"Ugh, he hates closed doors." Danny let him out, but warned, "That's it, Jonesy, you're out for good."

"So, your mom seems friendly, too. Must run in the family."

"Yeah," said Danny. "She's generally a nice person. I think she was also relieved to see that I had a friend over. It's been quiet here lately."

Kevin continued inspecting Danny's bedroom. His interest in learning about him made Danny feel special.

Kevin didn't question why there were two bureaus there, or why one corner of the room was empty and the other was crammed with posters, piles of dirty clothes, empty Coke cans, and other bric-à-brac.

"Did you get your textbook yet?" Danny inquired.

"Yeah, but I forgot to bring it. We can just use yours, right?"

"Sure."

Danny couldn't believe Kevin was here.

If last night hadn't happened, he would have been flustered, struggling to play it cool, to say the right things and not embarrass himself. Instead, he had plenty to say and only felt flashes of nervousness between his nagging thoughts of Nancy and Madam Maggie.

"Can I take my shoes off?" Kevin asked.

"Oh, yeah, sure. Get comfortable."

After tearing his boots off, Kevin picked up Danny's sketchbook from his nightstand and flopped onto the bed next to Danny.

"Oh, er, that's my sketchbook."

Kevin smiled. "I know."

He flipped through several pages of portrait sketches—mostly celebrities that Danny had found in Rolling Stone—then Kevin stopped on the page with his first sketch of the hands and crystal ball.

"Wow, you're a great artist. Keep up the good work, Dan. Dan-the-Man."

"Thanks. I considered applying to art colleges, but I'm not sure I see a point anymore."

"Oh yeah? Hey, who's Tommy? Is that your brother?"

Danny realized Kevin was reading his notes about Tommy and Madam Maggie that he scribbled in his sketchbook. He snatched the book out of Kevin's hands and slapped it shut.

"Uh… Sorry, I'm a little sensitive about that. My brother, Tommy, died earlier this year. Back in March. We should start studying now, anyway."

"No skin off my back if you don't want to talk about him," Kevin said. "But I wouldn't mind learning more about you."

"How did you know Tommy was my brother?"

"I guess someone at school told me. How did he

die?"

The question dropped like a bomb. Danny had never explained Tommy's death before. It seemed everywhere he went, everyone already knew.

"They say it was an accident. It was because of me, though. I mean, he died because I…" Danny trailed off and sighed.

"I know it's gotta be hard to talk about," said Kevin. "But you can tell me." He took up one of Danny's hands and caressed it.

The room seemed to spin, swirling together the conflicting ecstasy of Kevin's gentle touch and the painful memory of Tommy's tragedy. The two things seemed bound together, one dependent on the other. Danny didn't want to disappoint Kevin, so he continued…

"I told him he was weak—we were fighting. He got upset and left and I don't remember much else. The next day, he was dead. They said it was accidental, but I'm not sure. I…"

Kevin snuggled up to Danny on the edge of the bed and put his arm around Danny's shoulders.

The butterflies in his stomach churned as he swooned over Kevin's closeness. He couldn't believe it was happening. The thing he had fantasized about for years was happening. It felt unreal. A dream.

But what if his mom saw them like this? She wasn't

the type to barge into his room without knocking, unlike his dad. His dad would disown him if he saw this. But he was gone. Not a concern anymore. Still, what if his mom came in?

Danny shot up off the bed, intending to lock the bedroom door, then realized how bad that would look to Kevin. Why would someone lock the door on a friend? But he was turning out to be more than a friend. Maybe it made sense. But his mom would be suspicious of a locked door. How would he explain that?

Oh stop overthinking, damnit!

"Maybe, uh, we could put some music on after all," Danny said. "Just for a while before we study."

Danny's hands shook gently as he retrieved the Gene Loves Jezebel record from the crate and set it on the platter.

As Jay and Michael Aston began to sing about sugar and honey, Danny remained at the stereo with his back to Kevin, unsure what to do. He was making a fool of himself.

Just when he thought his trepidation would make him faint, a hand touched his shoulder. It glided over his arm, down to his wrist, into his own hand, then pulled him around to face Kevin.

Kevin's gorgeous mouth was so close now, and he fixated on it. The electric pull of attraction brought them closer, until Kevin leaned in to close the gap and their lips touched. Danny responded with a deep, passionate kiss. His first genuine kiss.

Danny let his hands explore Kevin's toned body over his clothes.

He had fallen into another realm now, where suffering dissolved and pleasure prevailed. There was nothing else. It was poetry. It was a thousand roses blooming at the same moment. It was—

Kevin pulled away.

"Danny, I'm sorry you had to go through that. Maybe I could, you know, be here for you."

What? Whiplash.

"Oh, yeah, okay."

"My sister split this world when I was seven years old."

"Oh, geez, that's intense."

The fog lifted. Back to reality. Stupid, painful reality.

"She committed suicide."

"Kevin, that's awful. She was your big sister?"

"Yeah. Ten years older than me."

Ill-equipped to face his own grief, let alone someone else's, Danny floundered and let awkward silence creep in. Should he tell Kevin more about Tommy? The pressure to say something mounted. Gah.

Kevin smiled. "You don't have to say anything else. I'm just glad we found each other."

Kevin pulled him closer. With Danny's head resting on his shoulder, Kevin's arms enveloped him, and they hugged each other tightly.

11

DREAM I

*D*anny walked along the old wooden pier with Tommy at his side. He squinted as the sun beat down on them. The hot wooden planks of the pier warmed his feet with every step. Now and then, a gentle breeze rolled off the top of the water surrounding them, a relief from the heat. The sounds of calliope music, screams, and laughs faded the further they moved from the lively boardwalk behind them. The pier reached so far out over the glistening water that there was no end in sight.

"Where are we going?" asked Tommy.

"Terminus," answered Danny.

A portentous feeling washed over him. The bright sun and cloudless blue sky became sinister, the crystal-clear water a mysterious, looming threat.

"What is Terminus?" asked Tommy.

"It is this," said Danny, pointing.

And there it was, the end of the pier.

"Oh, I see," said Kevin.

Danny blinked in confusion. Kevin's face smiled at him. Where did Tommy go?

Oh wait, I'm Tommy now.

Okay, so this is a dream. I'm dreaming.

Tommy/Danny stepped forward and looked over the edge of the pier. The surface reflected his image back at him. Through the clear cyan water, he could see all the way to the sandy bottom, a dozen feet below the surface. Two bright yellow fish chased each other, darting around waving green seaweed. A crab scurried away from a creeping shadow cast by a dark mass floating in the water above it.

"Terminus," said Kevin.

The dark floating mass twisted with the gentle current of the water and flipped over, revealing a face—a gray, lifeless human face, attached to a bloated male body suspended a few feet under the water. A dead man. The eyes were a cloudy, mottled white, and the mouth gaped open, a small moray eel peering out of it like a resident demon.

Actually, the water was full of dark masses, all like this one, all casting shadows on the ocean floor.

"Terminus," said Danny.

Where did Kevin go?

Danny peeled his shirt off. Tommy sensed he should do the same. Both boys stood shirtless, ready for the grim devastation that he somehow knew was their destiny.

Danny pushed Tommy into the water.

Thrashing his arms and legs as he hit the surface, Tommy felt his leg and arm brush against one of the dead bodies as he struggled to stay afloat.

Danny leapt into the water after Tommy.

With a crushing grip on his head, Danny used both hands to push Tommy under the water. Tommy yielded to the force, thinking, *I will give you what you want.*

Why isn't he fighting? wondered Danny. *Why is he giving up so easily?*

Tommy felt a writhing, slippery eel encircle his leg.

"Breathe!" Danny shouted. "Breathe!"

Tommy was confused. *But I'm under water!*

"Breathe!"

And then Tommy knew what to do. He opened his mouth and, with one powerful inhalation, filled his lungs with water. Adrenaline flooded his body, and his arms and legs thrashed around involuntarily. The eel moved up his body, over his chest, around his neck...

Danny wrestled with Tommy for a while, until finally, his body went limp.

Two become one, he thought.

Two become one.

I am one...

12

BATHROOM BREAK

*D*anny shifted and stirred awake as bits and pieces of the previous night coalesced in his groggy mind. After making out for a while, Danny and Kevin had tried to study for the quiz as planned, but there were more tempting activities vying for their time, like cuddling.

Danny could remember giving in, laying on the bed with Kevin, and eventually dozing off with his head on Kevin's chest. He told himself that ditching the study session was okay. This was a momentous event in his life—making out with someone for the first time, ever. If it costs him an *A* in US Government, so be it.

But Danny had no recollection of Kevin leaving. He didn't write a note, like they do sometimes in the movies. There was no evidence at all of Kevin's visit.

Was it all a dream?

Well, it did seem too good to be true. When Danny looked at himself in the mirror, he knew he wasn't *un*attractive. Still, Kevin felt out of his league. Beautiful hazel eyes, a handsome face, that naturally toned body, his friendly personality and cool confidence—all things that Danny lacked. Maybe it was Kevin who was dreaming, bound to wake up and see Danny for what he was, and then, of course, kick him to the curb. Stupid insecurity.

Maybe he shouldn't make any assumptions about what it meant, anyway. Kevin could have been overcome with emotion as he and Danny talked about the deaths of their siblings, and he might now regret what happened. That what happened between them could have been meaningless made Danny feel dirty.

The old flip clock on his nightstand read 6:20 a.m.

Danny rushed to get ready for school. He needed to allow some time before homeroom to cram some studying in.

As he made his way through the dark halls to his locker, he sensed something was wrong. There weren't many people in school yet, but the ones already there gave him strange looks. Kristy Farrow, who he'd never spoken to in his life, rolled her eyes and made a disgusted face at him as they crossed paths. Further down the hall, his lab partner from junior year, Shonda Miller, turned her head away when Danny said good morning to her.

Danny swung his locker open and faced the mirror on the back of the metal door. He checked himself for anything bizarre. Okay, no bits of breakfast stuck to his cheek, or pen ink smeared on his nose, or anything out of place at all. His hair was always kind of a mess, so nothing odd there. He fussed with a few strands of it, then a flash of movement in the reflection behind him startled him.

He jumped back and whirled around, but nothing was there. The hall was empty, both ways. He stood motionless for a moment, listening. A locker slammed somewhere in the building, a car beeped outside, but nothing else.

What was that? He must be going crazy. Unless it was the darkness again.

Danny turned to face his locker and shrieked.

Tommy!

In the mirror!

No. It was Danny's own reflection.

He slammed the door shut, feeling like a fool, and headed toward his homeroom.

Maybe he had read too much into the girls' behavior. He decided it was best not to dwell on it.

When he arrived at his empty homeroom classroom, he sat in one of the hard plastic chairs with shiny chrome legs and pulled out his notes for Mr. O'Quinn's class from his book bag.

Ten minutes later, engrossed in pre-revolutionary history, Danny jumped at the sound of his name.

"Danny!"

Angela was beckoning him from the doorway. "Come here. I need to show you something."

"Ange, I need to study for this government quiz."

Angela stomped over to Danny, grabbed him by the arm, and pulled him out of his seat.

"Ow, what gives?" cried Danny

"You're gonna want to see this…"

Danny tensed and resisted as she pulled him into the hall, then toward the entrance to the girls' bathroom.

"Whoa, wait! I can't go in there," he said.

Danny's shoes squealed as he dug in his heels, but Angela was strong and pulled him into the bathroom.

Elizabeth Mack, with her enormous glam metal hair, gasped when she saw him. "Ew, I guess you really are a creep. Get out!"

"Take a chill pill, Miss Mack," said Angela. "I dragged him in here. And you know why."

Elizabeth rolled her eyes and left.

It only took a moment for Danny to see it. It was hard to miss, on the center mirror, written in bright red:

Who attacked Nancy Biddle?

And underneath:

Danny Douglass

Stunned, Danny's mouth hung open.

Angela crossed the bathroom and pulled the lever on the towel dispenser, but nothing came out.

"Lipstick. We have to get this off before anyone else sees it. This bathroom is going to be full of girls in about ten minutes."

She pushed her way into a stall and pulled a long strand of toilet paper off the roll. "Here," she said, tearing it in half.

Danny took a piece, applied some hand soap, and wiped at the lipstick, but it just smeared.

"We need alcohol," he said, "or nail polish remover. Why would someone do this?"

"Obviously, someone thinks you had something to do with Nancy's injuries." Angela furiously rubbed at the lipstick with her wad of toilet tissue. "If we can at least make it illegible, that will be good enough."

"Nancy is an idiot. I never liked her anyway."

Angela paused and glared at him. "Danny, I'm

going to ask you something, and I will never, ever bring it up again… Did you hurt Nancy?"

The bathroom door swished open, and a freshman girl walked in.

"GET OUT!" Angela screamed at her.

Startled, the poor girl turned and left without a word.

"Angela, are you kidding me?"

"Just say it, Danny."

"No, I didn't. I would never hurt anyone," he blurted out…but it didn't exactly feel honest to say. He had hurt Tommy, hadn't he?

Sometimes people don't mean to hurt others, but they do. Maybe Danny was so wrapped up in his thoughts after Maggie's reading that he hadn't noticed Nancy coming out of the Hall of Mirrors.

"Not intentionally, anyway," he added.

Angela returned to scrubbing.

"All I mean is that Nancy can get herself into trouble without my help. She was drunk. And she's annoying. That's all."

"She didn't deserve to be attacked."

Danny went back into the stall and pulled out another length of toilet paper. "No, she didn't deserve it."

By the time his name was smudged beyond recognition, Danny's hands were stained with red lipstick.

"I should go now," he said. "My presence in the girls' bathroom isn't helping my case any."

"Okay, go. Lay low, and let's meet for lunch on the north lawn so we can discuss damage control."

Danny nodded and headed next door into the boys' bathroom to wash his hands. As he turned the corner, a wave of terror seized him.

Scrawled in black lipstick this time, on the center mirror, he read:

Who killed Tommy Douglass?
Danny Douglass

The bell rang.

"Pencils down!" said Mr. O'Quinn.

Danny failed to finish the quiz. He had no choice but to hand over his paper with two questions unanswered, to a silent but smug Mr. O'Quinn. The disturbing events of the early morning had left no more time to study, so Danny knew for sure he would not ace this one.

"Hey stud," someone whispered in his ear. Kevin appeared at his side, and they headed out into the hall together.

"Shhh! Someone could hear you," said Danny.

Kevin had arrived in class just as the bell rang and was forced to sit in the back of the room, out of reach. Danny was glad to speak with him now.

"I don't remember you leaving last night."

"Ah, yeah. I'm sneaky. Were you heartbroken to wake up without me by your side?"

"Totally, like, devastated," Danny teased, kind of. Kevin's flirting with him was a good sign.

"Did you hurt yourself?"

"What?"

"You have a burn or something on your arm."

Danny twisted his arm up for a better look.

"Oh, uh, it's red lipstick."

Kevin raised an eyebrow. "Didn't know that was your type of thing. I mean, it's cool, I just—"

"No, it's... Look, I gotta run to meet my friend Angela for lunch on the North lawn. Why don't you join us, and I'll explain?"

"Okay, but I need to grab some lunch from the cafeteria first. I'll meet you there in a few minutes."

13
LUNCH

"*I* broke the mirror," explained Danny. "I panicked. I heard people out in the hall, and I thought they were coming in and I...threw the metal trash bin at it, and it shattered."

"Holy shit," said Angela. "You could get slapped with destruction of school property. Not to mention seven years of bad luck. Ha! Did anyone see you?"

"No. I mean, someone saw me leave the bathroom, but no one saw me do it."

"Did you clean it up?"

"Most of it fell into the sink, so I scooped it into the trash bin using some paper towels. There were two big pieces stuck in the frame still, and I pulled them out."

"Christ, Danny."

"I'm fine. I didn't cut myself. No one will know anything."

Danny didn't mention that the message in the boy's bathroom was different from the one in the girls' bathroom. It pained him to think about it, let alone say it out loud. In fact, he had only ever said it to Dr. Hughes, and she didn't seem to take him seriously.

Who else knew that he killed Tommy?

Angela and Danny sat on a grassy area on the north side of Woodside High School, where seniors sometimes converged during lunch. Patches of grass were fading into a straw-like brown. It was almost too chilly to be outside for lunch anymore.

Angela pushed her black sunglasses up to the bridge of her nose with one finger, then ripped open her small bag of Cool Ranch Doritos. "Why would someone say that about you? Do you have enemies I don't know about?"

"No," Danny assured her.

Danny opened his brown paper bag and pulled out a ham sandwich. His stomach turned a bit, so he shoved it back into the bag.

"Oh, here comes Kevin," he said.

"Who?"

Kevin trotted toward them with a square piece

of pizza in his hand, one large bite missing from the corner. "Tastes like cardboard," he said as he approached. "Good thing I'm not picky."

"Ange, this is Kevin, from my government class."

Kevin dropped to the ground between them.

"Uh, hi," she said. "Does he need to be here right now?"

Angela could be a snob and a jerk to people she didn't know, but Danny secretly loved it. It made him feel special that he wasn't filtered out.

"It's okay, he's my…"

"Friend," Kevin finished, "You know, from class."

Did he mean that, or was he just being discreet?

"Yeah, a close friend, though, and it's okay if he hears what we're talking about. He already knows some stuff. About Nancy."

Angela didn't respond, just crunched her Doritos. That meant she'd tolerate him.

Danny rehashed the morning's events for Kevin, who continued to eat his pizza in silence, nodding and squinting to suggest either his understanding or concern. Finally, Kevin said, "No matter how you look at it, that's pretty screwed up, isn't it?"

"Ange, do you think Claudia knows about it?"

"Oh, yeah," Angela answered. "I talked to her during third period. Although she didn't come right out and say so, I think she believes it. I think she suspects you had something to do with the attack. She resents that you don't get along with Nancy."

Could Claudia be the one that wrote the lipstick messages? She was difficult to read sometimes, and wasn't at all confrontational, but could she be that conniving?

"We need to figure out who did it," Angela said. "We can't have Claudia spreading her suspicions around school."

Danny was comforted by that. Angela had his back. Maybe she'd be open to his next idea...

"There is one thing that might help us," he said. "It's not a conventional thing, but uh, it maybe could help, if you guys are open to doing it with me. It's really, uh—"

"Spit it out," Angela snapped.

"Madam Maggie."

"Who?"

"She works the fortune-teller's tent at the carnival."

Angela served an incredulous look. "Those people are frauds, Danny. I was fine with you getting a reading that night, but we're in some serious trouble now. Nancy's in a coma and someone's spreading dangerous rumors about you in school. She couldn't possibly know anything about that and might even lead us down the wrong path."

"I don't think so," Danny protested. "When I talked

to her that night, she knew about Tommy, and she knew exactly how I was feeling. She knew my name without me even telling her. She's not a fraud."

Angela shook her head.

"I'm going anyway," said Danny, timidly asserting himself. "I've already set up another appointment with her. For a séance. To connect with Tommy on the other side. Tommy can help us."

"This is madness," said Angela.

Maybe she didn't have his back after all. He turned his head away, unable to look at her. How could she be so unbelieving? When it all turns out well, Angela will eat her words.

"I'll go." Kevin swallowed his last bite of pizza, then continued. "I'll go with you to the séance. It's worth a try."

Angela collected her purse and half-eaten lunch, then jumped up to leave. "You guys have a super time. I'm out."

14

SPIRIT BOARD

*T*here was nothing worse than being at odds with Angela. He'd only had a few serious squabbles with her over the years. Each time it was because Angela criticized something he did, or in this case, wanted to do. She could be rigid and cold in conflict, but the ice would always melt, eventually. Until then, though, he would be cut off, alone again, like he'd been for months after Tommy's death.

Danny formulated a way to patch things up with Angela. If he could find the answers he wanted without Madam Maggie, he could back out of the séance. Then he'd tell Angela he'd figured things out, and she wouldn't need to know why.

Danny parked his car at the end of a shabby strip mall on the edge of town—one that he'd passed hundreds of times. He looked around to make sure there was no one nearby who might recognize him, then slipped into Delphi, an occult shop.

Instantly, all his senses were engaged in a swirl of incense smoke, gentle New Age music, and store fixtures packed to the gills with mysterious and bizarre merchandise.

If Danny was going to raise the dead, he thought surely this would be the place to figure out how to do it.

"Hallo!" said the man behind the sales counter. He wore Coke-bottle glasses and had a long white beard that made him look like a wizard.

Danny nodded at the man, then meandered down an aisle of small metal dragons, gemstones, bottled herbs, and candles in all the colors of the rainbow. But none of that seemed quite right for his needs.

Books lined the back wall of the store. As Danny approached, he noticed two young women in conversation. One, wearing a heavy black cloak, leafed through pages of a book without even looking at it.

"I think if you cast a spell on your birthday, at the exact time of your birth, it's guaranteed to work," she said. "And if you're naked while you do it, like a newborn baby, it's even more guaranteed."

"Oh, definitely," said the other girl meekly. Her platinum hair was teased out miles away from her pinched, pale little face. "I'm sure of it. That's one thousand percent true."

"Have you tried it?"

"No, I always forget when it's my birthday."

"Oh. That's very odd for a Leo," said the cloaked woman.

The conversation stopped abruptly when they saw Danny.

He pretended not to notice them and scanned the rows of book spines in front of him, wondering if there were any about communicating with dead relatives.

"Hi," said a voice. "You're into vampires, eh?"

The cloaked girl with unnaturally black hair and icy blue eyes stood next to him now. She had a gold star sticker on her forehead, the kind teachers applied to student papers in elementary school. Did she know it was there?

"Uhm," Danny said. Then he realized his finger was touching a book about vampires.

"Vampires are much easier to kill in real life, you know. All those myths about a stake through the heart are just fiction perpetuated by fantasists. If you have a vampire problem, I know a guy."

"Oh, no, no, I was just browsing…for, well, a book

about spirits."

"Like, ghosts?"

"Er, well, maybe something about summoning… dead…relatives?"

"You shouldn't summon spirits. That's too dangerous for an amateur. You'll end up possessed, like Linda Blair."

How did she know he was an amateur?

"What if I'm already possessed?" he replied, only half joking.

The cloaked girl snorted. "As if! Ha, already possessed. You're funny."

Something about her made Danny uneasy. Her features were striking, unearthly even. But her nerdy laugh, the cloak, and the gold star were disarmingly ridiculous at the same time.

"Hallo!"

Danny whipped around to see the old man he'd passed when entering the store, hand outstretched. Danny offered his hand in return but recoiled at touching the man's flesh.

"I know. My hands are cold. I'm not dead, nor undead, I assure you—I just have poor circulation."

"Oh, okay."

"My name is Morgan. I overheard you saying that you were looking for a book on summoning spirits? I might be able to help you. Follow me."

The man led him down another aisle and whispered over his shoulder.

"Don't mind her. Zarene comes in here all the time, talks nonsense, wastes my time, and never buys anything. She's a fool."

Danny chuckled uncomfortably.

Morgan reached the end of the aisle, then pulled a flat box from a low shelf.

"This is a spirit board," he explained, tapping the front. "It's better than a book. It's a practical tool to help you communicate with the other side."

"You mean, like a Luigi board?"

"A Ouija board, yes. But Ouija is a specific brand name. We just call them spirit boards here."

"Ahh. My friend had one. I think she was just moving the little thing around herself, though. Do these actually work?"

"You must first believe that it will work, then it will. Spirits will only reach out to those who are receptive, those who will believe in them. Don't abuse the spirits by asking silly or insulting questions, either. They will just leave."

"I see," he said. "Well, I'll take it."

Danny handed over his cash, and Morgan processed the sale at the front register.

From somewhere deep in the shop, Danny could hear the cloaked young woman talking to someone else now.

"Sea glass is so much more powerful than quartz. Give it a try. You won't regret it," she said.

Morgan rolled his eyes, handing the purchase over to Danny.

"Have a nice day!"

Danny poked his finger through the plastic shrink wrap and ripped it away from the oblong box in one tug. He shimmied the cardboard lid off, then lifted the glossy spirit board out. Danny threw the empty box aside and set the board and the planchette on the desk in his bedroom.

He had already lit some white pillar candles and incense, and had meditated for a few minutes, so he was ready, finally. He'd waited all afternoon until it was dark, for the right mood, and until his mother had retired to her bedroom for the night, just in case something happened.

He surveyed all the characters and words on the board. Hello, Goodbye, Yes, No, the entire English alphabet, and numerals. There were also images of a sun and a moon.

Where should the planchette be placed to start?

Maybe on Hello?

Hmm.

Madam Maggie would know what to do. Should he

just go to her? No.

Danny retrieved the box and found a small pamphlet with instructions inside. Aha! Start on the letter *G*.

He placed the planchette on the board, touching it gently with fingers from both hands. He took a deep breath, sat in silence for a time, then asked, "Tommy, are you here?"

He watched the planchette with eager eyes.

It did not move.

"Tommy, if you are here with me, please give me a sign."

Silence, stillness.

He studied the board again, cast in a warm amber glow from the candlelight in his room. He watched the edge of the planchette and waited for the tiniest movement, but none came.

Talk to me, Tommy.

He waited a few quiet minutes. The refrigerator's soft electric hum emanated from the kitchen down the hall. The scent of his Egyptian sandalwood incense filled his nose with every breath.

He conjured an image of Tommy, remembered his cheery smile, his infectious laugh, and that pensive, droopy face when something concerned him.

Come to me, Tommy.

He also recalled the crushing look of disappointment aimed at him when he had wronged Tommy somehow. But Tommy's magnanimous nature was quick to forgive others' mistakes.

If only Tommy was as quick to apologize for his own mistakes...

He remembered when Tommy knocked him out of that oak tree at Grandpa's house. Danny's arm broke, and Tommy felt so guilty that he insisted on getting a cast along with Danny, just so they'd both suffer together. Tommy threw a fit when the doctor refused. Through all of it, the closest Tommy had come to actually apologizing for pushing him out of the tree was saying, "I'm sorry the doctor wouldn't give me a cast too."

People always asked them if they could read each other's minds. Danny would roll his eyes. They were twins, not superheroes or psychics. But sometimes Tommy moved through life as if the things left unsaid were already understood.

Danny needed a clear answer this time.

Come to me, Tommy.

Danny begged him to notice his pleas, to cross over and give him a sign.

The planchette did not move.

Was Tommy angry with him? Why would he not give him a sign?

A deep wave of sadness welled within Danny. The

crushing weight of emptiness pressed against his body, and tears pooled in his eyes, blurring his vision.

Tommy was gone. Really gone. And this wasn't working.

He closed his eyes, forcing tears to stream down his cheeks.

Don't give up. Refocus.

He visualized the vacuum of Tommy's death as a big black hole in his chest, sucking a current of energy into his feet, up through his legs, and redirected into his arms, and then hands, flowing out into the heart-shaped piece of plastic he was touching.

A transparent, ghostly double of the planchette detached from the solid object under his fingers and shifted away. It traveled across the board in a consistent, fluid motion and stopped at Hello.

"Tommy!" Danny's eyes shot open.

But there was no planchette on Hello. Only the one under his hands, still at the G. He'd only imagined it.

Danny's mind raced.

Okay, maybe it didn't actually move, but maybe Tommy's spirit had projected the vision of movement into his mind?

Danny closed his eyes again and envisioned the spirit board and the planchette.

"Tommy, if that was you, please give me another sign. Please say yes."

He imagined the river of energy still coursing through his body, his arms, his hands—then a shrill bell rang.

The telephone.

Danny had another sudden vision. The hands on the poster, with bolts of electricity between them. His pulse quickened and his breathing grew rapid.

Is Tommy calling?

Letting go of the planchette, Danny jumped from his desk and picked up the phone on his nightstand.

"Hello…?" he squeaked.

"Yes."

Stunned, Danny moved his mouth, but no words came out.

"Yes," said the voice on the other line, "I will go with you to the séance."

It was Angela, not Tommy.

"If you're going to do something this ridiculous," she said, "I figure it's better if I'm there with you."

15
SÉANCE

Although the midway was still lit up, it was mostly deserted. Staff members in blue sweatshirts locked and secured the hulking metal amusements and shuttered the concessions and games for the night.

Eleven o'clock was closing time, and Danny and Angela had arrived on the dot. They swept past the empty ticketing booths and headed to the back of the sprawl where Madam Maggie's tent was located.

"Here's your last chance," said Angela. "We can turn around now and still save your dignity."

"No," Danny answered firmly. "And if you're going to be here, please be open to the experience."

Aside from firming up the plans for the séance, Danny had talked little to Angela in the past week. He was sure that, somehow, her phone call and her "yes" was a sign from Tommy that he needed to go to the séance. He appreciated her change of heart, but he still sensed some bad blood. They only exchanged a few tentative words about superficial things when crossing paths in school. He could tell she was holding out, waiting to see how things went with Madame Maggie.

Maybe Angela was hoping things would go poorly enough that Danny would admit she was right. But that would not happen. Madam Maggie knew things, and he was expecting Angela to change her mind about that too.

The other explanation for Angela's stand-offishness was that she now saw Danny as a bad guy. Someone else in school certainly thought he was. If anyone else had seen the message in the boys' bathroom about being Tommy's killer, then it was possible Angela heard about it and knew what it said. Did she believe it?

As they finished threading their way through the carnival, Maggie's tent appeared before them, with Kevin hovering near the entrance, hands in his pockets.

Looking at the dark Hall of Mirrors next door,

Danny shuddered.

"Heyyyy." Kevin beamed as they approached.

Angela fake smiled as Danny hugged him.

Kevin had been pretty cool about going to the séance. They met on the north lawn almost every day for lunch, wondering together what it might be like to open a door to the other side. He never made Danny feel dumb for it, and even said that given the chance, he'd have a séance to contact his dead sister.

The curtain swung open, and Madam Maggie appeared.

"Thought I heard some talking. You're here! Good, you brought some friends. Come in, come in," she said, waving them inside.

The setup inside the tent was much the same as before, except there were three stools at the table this time. She must have known.

"Madame Maggie, these are my friends, Angela and Kevin."

Maggie smiled. "Have a seat, my dears."

She ambled her way to the chair with the carved wood frame, her garments and bangles swishing and clinking. Settling in, she opened a drawstring pouch and placed a small bell, an L-shaped rod, and a thin wood block on the table. Danny took the stool opposite her. Angela and Kevin filled in on either side.

"First things first. Have you got the money?"

"Yes," Danny said, dipping into his pocket for cash. He handed her a rolled up hundred dollars, hoping that Angela couldn't see the amount he was paying for a service she didn't approve of.

Maggie unrolled the bill and held it up to the candlelight, inspecting it for signs of counterfeit.

Danny bowed his head, but he could feel Angela's judgement boring a hole through him anyway.

"Many thanks, my child. Now, I want you all to take a deep breath, relax your bodies, and clear your minds. We will sit in silence for a minute as you adjust to the space around you. Close your eyes, if necessary. Quiet... Breathe..."

Danny followed Maggie's lead. The air inside was strangely warm. The amber glow of a single candle on the table softened the vibrant fabrics that layered the interior walls of the tent. He heard distant clanging from across the midway, but otherwise the atmosphere was calm and eerily silent.

"Now, Danny, please take up the items on the table... Good. Now fit the metal piece into the hole on the wooden base, and then hang the bell from the hook on the end. This is a spirit bell, which is used to communicate with spirits on the other side."

"Okay," said Danny. "How does it work?"

"I will ask questions of the spirits. One ring of the bell is a No, two rings mean Yes."

Danny checked on his friends. Both Angela and Kevin had grave expressions, surely for different reasons.

"Let us begin with a prayer. Heavenly light and power, we ask that you protect us and bless the spirit whose grace and attention we seek this evening. Let us all now join hands."

Everyone slid their hands onto the table and joined them, as Maggie had asked. Kevin's hand was warm, comforting. Danny gave it a squeeze and Kevin squeezed back. For a fleeting moment, it distracted Danny from his purpose, and he imagined curling up with Kevin in a tender embrace, far from any worry.

"Now, Danny, I want you to think of the deceased. What was his name?"

"Tommy. Tommy Douglass."

"Right, think of Tommy. Angela and Kevin, I want you to settle yourself into a welcoming state. Open your hearts and your minds to receive Tommy into our circle."

Maggie paused.

Angela's hand was limp and lifeless in his. Danny almost wished she wasn't there, with her cynical, negative energy polluting the area.

"Danny, recall Tommy's face, his personality, and concentrate on your memory of him."

Danny complied. When a minute had passed, the

grief welled within him again, as it so easily did.

The group was quiet.

Danny returned to the vision of a black hole in his chest, the manifestation of his loss. He imagined harnessing its power again and turning it into a vacuum, sucking energy from the ground, through his feet and upward. It passed into his arms and out through his right hand, into Kevin's, then Maggie's, then Angela's, then back into his left hand, and circled through the group again, trapped in a loop.

Gently, Madam Maggie whispered, "Tommy, are you present?"

After an agonizing five seconds, the small bell jingled.

Danny gasped.

Another jingle followed, indicating Yes.

"Tommy, thank you for joining us. Are you willing to answer some questions from us this evening?"

Jingle. Jingle.

Angela's face was stone, unreadable.

"Tommy, are you the brother of Danny, uh, Douglass?"

Jingle. Jingle.

"Tommy, are you at peace in the spirit world?"

Jingle…

Danny winced, squeezing tears out of his eyes.

"Is it because you were murdered?" asked Madam

Maggie.

"Excuse me?" Angela interjected, standing. "I've had about en—"

"Sit the FUCK down," hissed Kevin, anger engulfing his face like a wildfire.

Danny pulled on Angela's hand, still in his grasp. "Please," he pleaded.

Looking stunned, and probably intimidated by Kevin's sudden break in civility, Angela fell to her seat again.

"Tommy," continued Maggie, "were you murdered?"

Jingle. Jingle.

There it was.

"I'm sorry," said Danny.

"Do you seek justice before you can be at peace?" said Maggie.

Jingle. Jingle.

"Is there something I can do to help you?"

Jingle…

"Is there something Danny can do?"

Jingle. Jingle.

Maggie hesitated, glaring across the table at Danny.

"What can I do? Anything! Please, I just want my brother to love me, to forgive me. Oh God, what can I do?"

"Tommy…do you see the darkness that I see inside Danny?"

The warmth in the tent vanished.

Jingle. Jingle.

Danny shivered uncontrollably.

Maggie's head bowed towards the table. A raspy, guttural moan emanated in waves from her open mouth.

"Ooouuugh… Ooouuugh…"

Jingle. Jingle.

"No," said Angela. "I'm done."

Jingle jingle jingle jingle.

She released Danny's hand.

"You broke the circle!" he wailed.

Madam Maggie's head jerked up and back, her eyelids fluttering, drool slipping out of her wide open mouth.

"Aaaaaauuuugh!"

Her body quaked with increasing force.

The table launched up two feet, narrowly missing Danny's face, then crashed back down, knocking over the spirit bell.

Angela shrieked.

Maggie drew in a breath.

"Daaan-neeeugh," Maggie howled in an unnaturally youthful voice, much resembling his own.

"What the hell is that…? Oh my God," said Kevin. "Is that Tommy inside Madam Maggie?"

"Yes," said Madam Maggie in her new teenaged

voice. "Yes. Yes."

"Tommy, is that you?" Danny asked.

"Yes, Danny. I'm here, Danny. I don't have much time. You must meet me in the Hall of Mirrors."

"What?"

"You need to help me. I am lost," said Maggie. "Meet me in the Hall of Mirrors on the last night of the carnival, at eleven o'clock. Help me, and all will be resolved."

Maggie exhaled, her body went limp, and the séance was over.

16
AFTERMATH

Danny pulled up to Angela's house, only a few blocks away from his own, and stopped his car at the bottom of the walkway. Shock and adrenaline coursed through him still, making his body twitch and shiver in spurts.

Angela didn't get out of his car. She stared ahead blankly, as she had the entire way home.

"We're here, Ange."

She said nothing.

Danny put the car in park and turned the ignition off.

Eventually she would say something. Maybe it'd

be "I'm sorry for doubting you." How could she deny what they'd experienced? If not, if it was a lashing of some sort, maybe their friendship would be over. Whatever. At least he had Kevin now.

Kevin...

Kevin's outburst at Angela shocked Danny. That he cared enough to get upset also charmed Danny. He had defended him and refused to allow anyone to get in the way of what was important to him.

Why couldn't Angela just support him? She was always interfering. She wasn't his mother. He didn't need another mother.

"Did you leave something in my car the last time we went to the carnival?"

"What?" she said, breaking her silence.

"The night that Claudia was attacked. I drove you home, and later found something here, on the front seat. Is it yours?"

"I didn't leave anything in your car, Danny."

"Okay. Are you going to leave, or are you just gonna stay in my car all night? If so, fine, but I'm going to drive back to my house and get in my warm bed."

The words hung in the air a moment too long and soured.

"Do you realize, Danny, that you still haven't talked about the night Tommy died? I mean, I know what happened. Everyone knows the basic facts. But I've never heard it from your perspective." She broke her empty gaze and turned to face him. "What do you know about how he died?"

Danny's instinct was to deflect, but he knew Angela's patience was running thin. What did it matter now?

"I…"

A bottleneck of memories overwhelmed him, and Danny didn't know what to say, where to begin.

"We… Uh…"

"Start from the very beginning," said Angela.

"Okay. Well, uh, I guess everything was fine that day. It was a normal day. We were having dinner—I remember it was tuna casserole—and…"

17

HOW THE OTHER HALF DIES

*D*anny was ravenous, but first drank his whole glass of water before sitting down at the dining table. He went into the kitchen to fill it up again, then rejoined his family at the table.

The Douglass family ate dinner every night at 6 p.m.—except that night.

Danny had ventured into the woods behind their house for a hike after school, something he only did when he had a bad day. The towering trees, the quiet, and the smells of nature all calmed him, and sparked his imagination, until whatever worried him melted away. The dirt path he'd followed was once clear and well-worn, but as the twins had grown older and ventured out less, it narrowed as nature reclaimed it. He walked all the way to the creek that day, and on the way back he stopped at the old treehouse, remembering their younger days.

Danny had lost track of time. When he'd returned, he was ten minutes late for dinner. He knew better.

Mom had insisted they all wait for his return, and now an icy tension filled the air as they began eating.

"Sooooo, how was your day at school?" Mom ventured, always the peacemaker.

"Good," said Tommy.

"Danny?"

"Fine."

Dad cleared his throat. "Tommy, did you meet with Dr. Hughes today?"

"Oh, yeah. She said my SAT score was high enough that I wouldn't have to take it again, but I told her I probably would anyway."

Danny knew what was coming. The elephant in the room would be addressed in 3, 2, 1...

"Danny, do you think you might reconsider—"

"No, Dad."

"It's okay, James," Mom said. "The schools on Danny's list don't factor SAT scores into their decisions."

She couldn't even bring herself to say art schools.

Dad's eyes launched daggers of disapproval. "Oh, he has a list now, does he?"

Danny's face flamed red.

"Yeah," said Tommy. "And there is some overlap with my list."

"No, there's not," Danny corrected.

"Well, you mentioned Cal Arts."

"That's strictly an art school. It doesn't have a journalism major for you."

"I might want to start in a photography program, though."

"Huh?" Danny dropped his fork. "You have never mentioned that before. It's been your plan for years to go to Columbia, for journalism."

"It was more a dream. I'm keeping my options open."

"Apparently only since I said I would never go to Columbia in a million years."

"You weren't always against it. Columbia has art. I don't know why you wouldn't want to go."

But they all knew the answer to that. It wasn't that he wouldn't go. He couldn't. His GPA and his SAT scores weren't good enough. He was never the type of student that would survive the rigors of an Ivy League school. Not because he wasn't smart enough, but because, as his father pointed out repeatedly, he never "applied" himself. Well, maybe his father should stop dwelling on what Danny could be, and see who he actually was. Danny had made peace with that part of himself, and with being away from his brother, with forging a separate path.

In fact, he welcomed it. There were things Tommy didn't know about him yet, things that he needed to explore on his own, things that no one in his family would understand or accept. Like the feelings he had for other boys. He didn't need the prying eyes of his twin getting in the way.

"It's perfectly okay if we don't go to the same school, you know."

Dad pointed his fork at Danny. "It would be easier on your mother and me if you went to the same school," he said. "I think you should take the SAT again, Danny. Columbia is close to home."

And that's another reason Danny didn't want to go there.

"Let him be, James. They'll figure out what's best."

Dad eyed Mom over his glasses and chose not to say anything.

"May I be excused?" Danny asked, disgusted.

"Life is difficult, Danny. Difficult conversations, tough decisions. Can't always run from them. Better get used to it," said Dad.

Danny hated him and his tough guy bullshit. Danny didn't feel weak. He felt he'd endured a lot and survived, but Dad didn't know or care to know.

"You're excused," said Mom.

Danny left a half-eaten dinner on his plate and retreated to their bedroom. He suspected they were still talking about him. Maybe they weren't. He felt like the odd one out, all the same. An outsider in his own family.

His parents didn't go to Ivy League schools. They had modest jobs in a blue-collar town. Why did they expect so much more from him?

Tommy was the golden boy, an overachiever, a people pleaser, a generous friend, an obedient son, and Danny could never match up. Tommy was Dad's favorite now, it was obvious. And though their mother evenly distributed her love, she offered more sympathy, or pity maybe, to Danny, which had an ironic effect on his self-esteem. Poor, poor Danny.

Well, he'd had enough.

"I'm not going to Columbia," he said when Tommy joined him in their bedroom, "and I'm not going to any other school that you choose, for that matter. You should accept that reality now."

"We'll see about that."

"We don't always have to do the same thing, be the same person. In fact, we haven't always been. You're into photography and I like to draw. You're left-handed and I'm right-handed. You failed algebra freshman year, and I have never failed a class."

Tommy leaned against his bureau, arms crossed. "And now I'm acing AP Calculus and you're getting Cs in Geometry," he teased, trying to lighten the mood, but only making Danny angrier.

"And let us not forget another difference between us—why Mom and Dad got us separate beds…"

"Danny, that's low."

"Because you were a bedwetter. Until we were eight years old."

Tommy frowned at him.

"And I have never, ever, wet the bed," Danny added.

"Yeah, I get it," said Tommy. "We're different. Believe me, I know we are, and I'm okay with it. But that doesn't mean we should go to different schools. Try to think about what's best for the entire family. Dad has a point."

Tommy's refusal to recognize the fire aimed at him made Danny's blood boil. Tommy needed to feel some pain, damnit.

"You're codependent," Danny snarled.

"You better stop while you're ahead. I am not codependent."

"You cried yourself to sleep for a month after we got separate beds," Danny continued. "You got a scholarship to a photography camp last summer but backed out like a wuss because you'd have to spend three weeks without me. We've never spent a single night apart in our entire lives! Sometimes I wish you would back off and give me some space. Sometimes you make me sick. I wish you weren't such a weak little—"

"Watch it, Danny." Tommy dropped his arms, clenched his fists.

"Anyway, it wouldn't be a lie to say you have... an addictive personality. Would it? That's another thing that makes us different. I don't have a drinking problem."

Danny hit the mark, hard.

It had never been spoken aloud. But Danny had noticed the empty bottles buried deep in their closet, had smelled it on him. He knew Tommy was sneaking out in the middle of the night. And Danny said nothing about it. But it was out in the open now.

"You're an unbearable prick," Tommy fumed.

"I'd rather be a truthful prick than a codependent bitch."

"I am not codependent."

"Prove it. Spend one single night away from me. Go...sleep in the treehouse. Tonight."

Tommy took a deep breath, then calmly picked up his backpack and started shoving things into it, including a bottle of whiskey that he didn't even bother to hide this time.

Then he left.

Danny was satisfied. Tommy had a way of dismissing his feelings when they conflicted with his own. A statement was made. Tommy couldn't sweep this one away; he would have to accept it. Would have to accept that their futures were going to be separate.

Though…he wondered if he'd gone too far. Oh well. Whatever it takes.

Danny woke up the next morning to his mother shaking his shoulder.

"Where is Tommy? Danny, wake up."

He had grumbled something or other when she had knocked on their bedroom door earlier to tell them it was time to get up. It was a school day.

After a few moments, Danny registered what she was saying. And then he remembered the argument.

Tommy's bed was empty and made-up like he hadn't slept in it. He never came back.

"Uhhh…I don't know."

"Well, was he in here last night? He's not in the house. Where could he be at this hour?"

"I'll find him," said Danny.

That seemed to suffice for the moment, and Mom continued with her morning routine.

Danny didn't have time to trek a quarter mile into the woods behind their house to see if Tommy had actually slept in the tree fort. Despite what happened, he was certain Tommy would show up at school. He had never let his little problem interfere with his schoolwork.

And why should he rescue his brother, anyway? If Mom and Dad were angry with Tommy, so be it. He should feel the full pain of being a disappointment to his parents, just like Danny had felt for years.

Danny, having decided not to look for Tommy and to let him suffer the consequences of his actions, grabbed the box of Ghostbusters cereal from the pantry and poured a bowl for himself.

Mom and Dad were in their bedroom talking.

"I can't leave for work until I know he's okay."

"He'll be grounded for a week."

"What if something happened to him?"

"He didn't tell us he was leaving. He must have snuck out for a good time. He'll be grounded for a month, don't worry, Susan. Trust me, he will never do it again."

"No, I'm calling the police."

Danny shot up and put the milk back in the fridge, leaving his cereal dry.

Punishment from Mom and Dad was one thing, but Danny feared what might happen if the police found Tommy with alcohol. Would he be arrested?

"Wait...I think I know where he is," said Danny,

standing in their bedroom doorway.

Two minutes later, wearing a winter coat over his pajamas, he left through the back door, made his way across the frosty back lawn and into the woods.

Damnit.

Danny told him to leave, so he suspected this whole thing would backfire on him. As always, Tommy would emerge squeaky clean. So much for putting his foot down.

The bitter cold nipped at his ears and fogged his breath.

He trudged along the overgrown dirt path in his moccasin slippers, recalling his hike before dinner the previous night. If he had known then an argument with Tommy would put him right back out here at 6:30 a.m. (and probably now make him late for school), would he have let it escalate like it did?

The brisk air seeped into his pajamas at his bare ankles and sent shivers up his body. He stuffed his hands in the pockets of his puffy black coat and pulled it closer.

There were no blankets in the tree fort. Tommy left yesterday wearing his heavy coat, but if he was there all night, he must have been cold.

That was his choice.

But…the thought of him sleeping out here alone, like a stray animal, was kind of pathetic.

Maybe it was Danny who was cold to force him out like he had.

Okay, but a point had to be made about college. Surely Tommy knew now how serious he was about going to separate schools.

Through a web of grey-brown branches ahead, a solid form took shape in the trees, a dozen feet above the ground.

Even if he and Tommy were to mend fences, they would still have to discuss the drinking problem. That might be tricky, a tough pill to swallow. Might go down easier if Danny opened up about his own secret. Was he ready to reveal that?

Danny surveyed the ramshackle tree fort, which looked like a hunting blind, thanks to some construction guidance from their father. They had built it themselves during the summer between 5th and 6th grades. He remembered lugging all the lumber supplied by their father to this perfect spot. The four walls and floor were still intact, but the flat plywood roof had rotted and disintegrated within the first couple of years, leaving open gaps to the sky.

At the doorway of the fort, above the two-by-four ladder, he could see a sliver of a sneaker peeking out.

Tommy was here.

Danny kicked the ladder, sending vibrations through the structure.

"Tommy, let's go. We gotta go to school now."

No response.

"Look, I probably said some things I shouldn't have. It looks like we both got some issues we need to discuss. Let's talk after school today."

Silence.

"Tommy!"

Danny climbed the ladder and grabbed Tommy's leg and tried to shake it, but the leg was stiff and didn't move.

He scaled a few more rungs on the rickety ladder and took in the full view of Tommy inside, folded into a fetal position, backpack serving as pillow, an empty bottle of whiskey at his side.

"Tommy?"

Danny leaned in and tried shaking his shoulder this time, but it was fixed in place, like a sleeping marble statue.

The early morning light coming through the holes in the roof provided just enough visibility for him to see that Tommy's face was a yellowish grey, his lips purple.

He was frozen solid.

Angela wiped away tears as Danny's account of that morning finished.

"His last words to me were 'You're an unbearable

prick.' Can you imagine? I forced him out, and he died. It was the cold that killed him—hypothermia accelerated by alcohol. I knew about the alcohol and didn't tell anyone. I killed him. I murdered my own brother."

Danny cupped his hands to his face and sobbed.

Angela climbed out of the car, slammed the door, and headed toward her house, leaving Danny alone again, blinded by his tears.

18

A FOX IN WOLF'S CLOTHING

*F*irst period art class on Monday mornings was a welcome transition between the weekend and the school week.

The class yawned, rubbed their eyes a lot, and didn't say much, which Danny appreciated.

Mrs. Donahue, who often played Miles Davis and Stravinsky for the budding artists on her quiet little cassette player, would float around the room, whispering "Excellent," "Congratulations," "Fine use of line here," "Oh my, have you considered cerulean instead?"

Despite the placid atmosphere that morning,

Danny's mind roiled with thoughts of the séance and the fallout with Angela.

Although dramatic and enthralling, ultimately the séance disappointed him. He expected answers but received none. If Madam Maggie had opened a line of communication with the spirit world, why was he directed to the Hall of Mirrors? Why couldn't Tommy just talk to him through her? Maybe it was Angela's bad juju that scared him off.

Angela's behavior that night baffled him. She was rarely without something to say. Her silence in the car on the ride home, and then when Danny shared his memory of Tommy's death, felt like an arrow through his heart, a knife in his back. He wanted to be sympathetic. After all, she had been friends with Tommy, too, and hearing the details of his death must have been difficult. But did she really have to ignore his pain? Again?

"Good morning, Danny," said Mrs. Donahue.

"G'morning," he replied.

"I was disappointed that I didn't see you at the first Portfolio Club meeting. Are you still planning to apply to art schools?"

Ugh, not this again.

"Probably, yeah."

"Our little club is a great resource for talented artists like yourself who need to build a portfolio for applications."

"I will try to make the next meeting," Danny lied.

"You have a great imagination, Danny. Don't waste it." Mrs. Donahue touched his shoulder and moved on to the next student.

Danny wanted to share his thoughts about the séance with Claudia, who always sat with him in art classes, but she was on the other side of the room that day. Her break with tradition surely signaled that she was rejecting him.

Claudia was absent from class last week, which seemed odd. According to Angela, she knew about the mirror messages before Danny did. That would place Claudia in school last Monday morning before homeroom, but then why wasn't she in first period art class? Strange.

Danny turned his attention to the project in front of him. The class were working on their papier-mâché Halloween masks they'd begun two weeks ago. He was making a werewolf mask and based his design on the main character from the movie *Teen Wolf*. His mask was already constructed and primed white. It just needed some color to bring it to life.

Michael J. Fox as a teenage werewolf.

Fox as wolf.

Danny mused on the idea.

He went over to the supply wall, poured brown

liquid acrylic paint from a plastic jug into a Dixie cup, and then did the same with yellow, white, and black.

He glanced at Claudia periodically, but she refused to make eye contact.

Back at his workstation, Danny opened his sketchbook and flipped through, searching for the wolf sketches he'd done based on pictures from a *Teen Wolf* magazine feature. Before he found the right page, something caught his eye. Was that a full page of writing he just passed?

He flipped back a couple of pages and, sure enough, a full page of written words—something he never would have done in his sketchbook. He didn't remember writing anything here, but the handwriting was definitely his own.

I know that eventually this darkness I struggle with will kill me. While I am still here, I want to set the record straight.

I am not who you think I am.

I am a liar and a master manipulator.

Tommy's death was not an accident. He was starting to figure out who I was, so I got rid of him. When my parents were asleep, I lured him out into the woods, tied him up, forced him to drink until he passed out, then I left him there to die from exposure.

Nancy suspected the truth, so I had to do the same to her.

There will be others...

19
FAILURE

"*H*ey babe, how're you doing?"

Lost in thought, Danny didn't notice that Kevin had joined him.

But the word "babe" brought him back to reality, to Mr. O'Quinn's room, with a few minutes before the start of class.

Babe? That's a level-up.

He wanted to feel its warmth, but he was still unsettled by that page in his sketchbook. He wanted to rip the page out and tear it up into tiny bits, make sure no one ever knew about it. But he kept it—he needed to figure out how it had gotten in there.

"Sorry, I'm a little distracted."

"Well, yeah, I bet you are," said Kevin. "That was some séance, wasn't it?"

"Oh, yeah…but afterward, Angela and I…had an argument, I guess you could say. We're not talking right now."

Danny hesitated to disclose the true nature of their conflict that night. If Kevin knew he'd told Angela the full story of Tommy's death, that might invite pressure from Kevin to tell him, too. He wasn't ready to relive the entire thing, yet again, for Kevin's sake.

"Bummer. She never seemed on board with the séance anyway, so whatever, man."

"I know. She's my best friend. What's wrong with her?"

"Doesn't sound like a good friend to me."

Ouch. Kinda true, though.

"I can't lose my best friend, too."

That seemed to stump Kevin—for a moment, anyway.

"I'm here for you," he said.

Danny only smiled. Kevin was amazing, but could he really replace both Tommy and Angela?

Danny asked, "So, why do you think Tommy didn't just talk to me at the séance? Why did he tell me to meet him in the Hall of Mirrors?"

"Oh, that's easy. Because he's trapped there. That's

where he is."

"Huh?"

"They say that when someone dies, their soul can get trapped in a mirror if they don't cross over soon enough, like, if they're wandering around with unfinished business. That's why in the olden days they'd cover up the mirrors when someone died."

"But Tommy didn't die anywhere near a mirror."

"You sure?"

"Positive."

"Well, maybe his soul wandered somewhere there was a mirror."

The bell rang.

Mr. O'Quinn approached the podium at the front of the classroom. The students cut their chatter. He retrieved a stack of papers from a folder there and strolled up and down the aisles of desks, returning last week's quiz.

Danny's heart beat faster. He knew his test would have a terrible grade. Maybe he should change his name to Danny "C" Douglass.

"Jessica Shue," Mr. O'Quinn said, handing over her quiz. "You might want to loosen that headband next time you take a quiz. I think it's cutting off the blood flow to your head, sweetheart. This is a disappointment."

Danny's heart sank. Expecting his own

disappointment, he now feared Mr. O'Quinn would deliver it with humiliating commentary. He had enough to be anxious about. He didn't need this asshole of a teacher piling on.

Mr. O'Quinn dropped a quiz down on Kevin's desk, but instead of moving on to the next student, he stood above him, staring, not saying a thing.

Danny could see the quiz score in bright red ink.

A+.

"Sir?" asked Kevin.

Mr. O'Quinn remained there, silent, and with a glassy stare, one that spoke: How did you get an *A+*? How did someone like *you* get an *A+*? You must have cheated.

Well, how *did* he get an *A+*? They skipped their study session to make out, and the quiz was early the next morning.

Mr. O'Quinn turned in place and dropped a paper on Danny's desk.

F.

"Tommy, if this is a reflection of your attitude towards my class, the feeling's mutual."

Several giggles broke out around the room.

"My name is Danny."

"I don't care who you are, Mr. Douglass, you're still a failure."

A failure. The words boomed in his mind, like the

explosion of a missile he knew was coming but was helpless to prevent.

Mr. O'Quinn moved on to his next victim, but Danny was inside his head now, oblivious to his surroundings.

It was true. Danny was a failure. And now everyone in his government class knew it.

The sound of heavy breathing drew his attention back to Kevin, who was gripping the edges of his desk with both hands, white knuckled, veins popping in his neck. His gaze was fixed on Mr. O'Quinn, and he looked like an attack dog ready to pounce.

"Shhh," Danny hushed.

"This son-of-a-bitch needs to go," Kevin whispered. "Mr. O'Quinn doesn't deserve to be a teacher."

Kevin's protective reflex comforted Danny once again. At least someone in this world cared enough to acknowledge his pain, to look out for him. But he didn't want things to get worse.

"I can talk to Dr. Hughes about him, or Principal Escher," offered Danny. "I appreciate that you're looking out for me, but let it go for now...babe."

With a half-smile, Kevin nodded in agreement—a relief to Danny. He had more important things to worry about, like confession letters he couldn't remember writing.

After class, they parted ways, which always gave Danny a little jolt of anxiety. He just wanted to be with Kevin, endlessly, holding his hand, staring into his hazel eyes, touching his—

"Danny, wait up!"

Angela pushed through the dense crowd of students in the hall, trying to catch up with Danny. He hadn't talked to her since Saturday night. In fact, he'd been avoiding her at all costs. For a moment, he pretended not to hear her. *Take that, rotten friend.* But his curiosity got the better of him. What did she want? To apologize?

Without looking back at her, he stepped into the nearest classroom, the dark, empty science lab, then waited for her to catch up.

"What?" he demanded, as she slipped in.

"We need to talk."

"Do we? What could we possibly need to talk about? Is it how you're a callous bitch who bailed on me Saturday night?"

Angela disregarded the well-deserved burn. "Can we hang after school tomorrow?"

"No, tell me now what you want from me."

"I can't. I have class in three minutes. And I have a five-page paper to write tonight."

Danny turned to leave, but Angela grabbed his arm.

"Wait, wait. There's something I've been keeping

from you that I need to come clean about."

Danny wrenched his arm out of her grasp. "What, Angela?"

She kicked the doorstop holding the lab door open, and it swung shut, muffling the din of boisterous students and lockers crashing out in the hall.

Angela was shaking.

"I was with Tommy the night he died."

20

CONFESSION

*A*ngela, in her beat up black leather jacket and a black wool beret, waited for Danny on the front step of his house as he pulled up. Finally, the moment had arrived.

Angela had flatly refused to say more about being with Tommy the night he died and insisted that they meet after school the following day for a proper conversation. This gave Danny plenty of time to speculate.

Why hadn't she shared such an important piece of information about his brother's death? She must have done something that night she didn't want anyone to know about, and if she didn't want anyone to know, then it must have been bad.

She must have had something to do with his death. What else could it be?

In that case, it would make sense that Angela had been manipulating him and his life to keep her secret hidden.

She did always prefer to be in control of every situation, but lately, that part of her personality seemed to be even more pronounced, more desperate.

She tried to talk him out of going to the séance, then when he refused, she cut him off, only to decide later it would be better for her to be there. She was also reluctant to accept Kevin as his friend, maybe because he supported the séance idea.

Could she have been steering him away from fortune tellers and séances because she feared that her secret would be revealed? Maybe she was only pretending not to believe in them. Maybe she actually feared them because they made her feel like she could lose control of the narrative.

Maybe she was pushing so hard for Danny to get on with his life because the sooner Tommy's memory faded, the sooner she could be certain that her secret would stay buried forever.

Did she have something to do with Nancy's accident? Did Nancy know too much? Was it just a warning shot, or had she intended to kill her too?

Why was she telling the truth now?

Danny was confused. Everything seemed muddied in his head, a fog of conflicting thoughts and theories.

And there she was, sitting on his front step, dressed all in black, like a shroud of mystery and…evil incarnate.

Danny shuddered.

"Hi," Angela sighed.

Danny nodded once, unable to muster a verbal response.

He unlocked the front door and led her into the kitchen, where they both dropped into seats at the Formica-topped table.

"Is your mom home?"

Danny shook his head, no.

Angela's eyes wandered around the room. "It's weird to be in your house again. I miss you, Danny. It feels like we haven't truly been on good terms for a while now. Losing Tommy sucked. I don't want to lose you too."

Then you shouldn't have kept secrets from me, he wanted to say. *Then you should have been a better friend,* he wanted to say. But instead, he waited for her to say more. He wanted the upper hand in this battle.

"Are you giving me the silent treatment now? So, I'm sorry, okay? Is that what you want to hear? I screwed up."

"That's a start."

"I'm worried about you. I think you're getting into some shit that isn't good."

"You've already made that clear. I didn't invite you over so you could lecture me about my poor decisions. Get to the point. You know, about how you screwed up."

Angela sighed. "Well, Tommy came to my house that night. He was really upset. I didn't invite him in. My stepdad was home, and he would've given me hell about it—you know how he is. I tried to calm Tommy down, and we went for a walk.

"He took me to the tree house in the woods and he told me what happened between you two earlier. I stayed with him as long as I could. It was so goddamn cold that night. We both had a few swigs of Jack, kept each other warm until about eleven.

"Danny, I have to be honest. It wasn't the first time we went to the tree house. It was our spot for a while, actually. Tommy and me, we were more than just friends."

Danny let this sink in, the reality of the lie, how it made him a dupe. A clown. A useless third wheel in what was once a great friendship between the three of them. Only a friendship. But they had perverted it, crossed a line, made it lopsided. And the tree house, which was Danny and Tommy's, became someone else's.

Danny buried his face in his hands. "How long?" he grumbled.

"Only about a month."

"So that's why he was sneaking out at night? To be with you? Did you guys ever…?"

Angela was silent, aside from the nervous tapping with her finger on the tabletop.

"Christ."

"We didn't want you to be upset with us or we would have told you. No one else knew. But anyway, that night in the treehouse, Tommy broke it off with me."

"Why are you telling me this now?"

"Don't you see? You can't blame yourself for Tommy's death. Or else I'm just as guilty. I told Tommy to go home, and he promised me he would. By the time I left, his mood had changed. But I still left him alone in the woods with a bottle of Jack, and he died. If anyone was responsible for Tommy, it would have been the last person with him. That was me."

"I don't know, I don't know." Danny shook his head. It was too much to sort out. Would a murderer admit to being the last person to see him alive?

"Danny, despite what you think about that night, you don't have a darkness within you. Madam Maggie is a business, not a prophet, not a shrink. She's telling you whatever she can to get more money out of you."

"No. No, she knew things."

"Don't be naïve, Danny. You're using supernatural bunk to distract yourself from the truth—that Tommy is dead. You need to heal and move on. And I don't think you should go to the Hall of Mirrors."

"Everyone grieves differently. Who are you to tell me how to grieve for my brother? My twin brother! What the hell do you know about that?"

Almost as soon as the words passed his lips, he regretted them. Maybe she didn't know what *that* was like, but her father had died in a car accident when she was five years old. She was in the car too. She must know something about loss. But that didn't change anything; Danny was still angry.

Angela sighed. "Grieving is one thing, letting your life disintegrate because of your grief is another."

"That's not what is happening. If you were a good friend, you'd know that. I've been better lately. Kevin supports me. He gets it. His sister died when he was young and he said he'd have a séance for her, given the chance. People have séances. Some people are spiritual. If you were a good friend, you'd be more understanding."

"I don't give a damn about Kevin," she snapped.

"Then I don't give a damn about you."

"You don't mean that."

Danny wasn't sure if he did or not.

"Look, I've heard things about Kevin," said Angela.

Danny felt his face flush. Could someone know about him and Kevin? Did someone overhear them calling each other "babe"? It was none of their business.

"People lie," he said. "You should know that."

"Apparently, he was kissing someone."

"It's not a crime," he said, brushing off the allegation.

"Britney Burns," said Angela, obviously feeding him small morsels of information at a time, trying to detect the slightest of reactions.

"Okay," said Danny.

"So that means nothing to you?"

"Why should it? Guys kiss girls all the time."

"The story is that he ditched her after they hooked up. That's pretty horrible."

But did he go to a séance with her? Did he call her "babe"? Did it matter?

"Well, maybe I can talk to him about it," Danny offered. But that sounded dumb coming out of his mouth.

"Unless you have something else to confess," he added, "I think I'm done with this conversation. You can go now."

"Well, I tried," said Angela. "Would you at least let

me use your bathroom before I go?"

Her house was only a few blocks away. Why?

"I've been holding it a long time."

"Fine."

Danny paced in the kitchen, ate an Oreo, and simmered in his loathing of her.

When she returned, Angela made for the front door, but on her way offered a warning:

"Danny, just so you know, I'm not done with you yet."

21
QUESTIONS

As soon as they were behind the closed door of Danny's bedroom, Kevin slipped his hands around Danny's waist and drew their bodies together. While his attraction to Kevin couldn't have been any stronger, troubling suspicions tempered it.

"I thought maybe we could do something else," said Danny, pushing away. "Maybe we could spend time getting to know each other for a while?"

"Oh, you don't want to make out again? I thought that's why you invited me over."

"I would really like that, but we're practically strangers still."

Kevin flopped on the bed. With his typical cheeky grin, he noted, "That wasn't a problem for you last time."

"Ugh, I know, I just thought—"

"Okay, okay, okay. I get it. What do you wanna know about me?"

"Let's play Twenty-One Questions?"

"Fine. You start."

Danny pulled up his desk chair and sat facing Kevin on the bed, who was unlacing his boots. "We'll alternate until we get to twenty-one. So, question number one: What's your favorite color?"

"Whatever color blue your eyes are," said Kevin, his own eyes beaming.

Danny could feel himself blush. How could he be anything other than perfect?

"Charming," said Danny. "Very charming. Your turn."

"Okay, question two: What's *your* favorite color?"

"Seems to change every year. Right now it's orange, I guess. Question three: The Smiths or The Cure?"

"Killing Joke."

"Don't be evasive," warned Danny.

"Well, I know better than to say The Smiths, so I'll go with The Cure. What's your favorite band? Question four."

"Siouxsie and The Banshees. Question five: Where

do you want to go to college?"

"You're assuming I want to go at all," Kevin scoffed. "I dunno what I want to do yet."

"Okay, I'll accept that answer."

"Good. Question six...uh... What's your favorite food?"

"Tacos. Question seven: Why are you living in a hotel instead of renting an apartment or buying a house?"

Kevin lifted an eyebrow at the shift to a more prying question. "Well, it was short notice, I guess. My parents didn't have time to find a place. Question eight—"

"It's been a month since school started," Danny persisted.

"Right. I don't know. They're working on it, I guess. Question eight: What is some place you'd like to go someday?"

"Hmmm. Madam Tussaud's wax museum. Question nine: Where are you from originally?"

"Woodside. We moved away and now we're back. Question ten: What did you first think of me?"

"You lived in Woodside as a kid? I don't remember you from school."

"Uh, I went to Carrol Elementary, not Woodside. Question eleven: What were you thinking when you first saw me?"

"I was thinking, 'Damn, he's cute. I hope I don't make an ass of myself.' Question twelve: Have you ever dated anyone before?"

"Nope. You're the first, Dan-the-man."

The answer surprised him. Kevin was, by all standards, very attractive. Sure, his style had an edgy, off-putting vibe to some, but he was still friendly and confident. Most guys like him would have had some kind of silly relationship by his age, even if it was a fake straight one in the 5th grade.

"Question thirteen," Kevin continued. "Have you told anyone about us?"

"Nope. Question fourteen: What's the worst lie you ever told?"

"I don't lie," Kevin asserted.

"Don't evade. Everyone has lied at least once or twice."

"Uh…I don't know. In that case, probably something stupid when I was young. Like saying I was sick just to stay home from school. Question… What question number are we at?"

"Fifteen."

"Question fifteen: What's your favorite part of my body?"

Easy one for Danny to answer. "Your lips. Question sixteen: Are you bisexual?"

"Nope. Question seventeen: What would you like to

do with my lips?"

"Draw them. Question eighteen: Have you ever lied to me?"

Kevin's face hardened. "I said I don't lie."

"Not even a little white lie? To me, I mean."

"Are you insinuating something? Why are you asking about lies? Do you not trust me?"

"I don't really know you. How can I trust you?"

"You know me well enough. I've never given you any reason to doubt me. You seem a little off today. You got something on your mind?"

Danny tensed. What a question. He always had something on his mind.

"Angela and I aren't speaking to each other again. I guess I'm feeling cynical about people right now."

Kevin's expression softened.

"Let's see if I can distract you from your worries. Question nineteen: What would you do if I got naked right now?"

Danny refused to let that thought distract him. Time to wrap this up.

"If you got naked, I would move on to the next question. Question twenty: Did you kiss Britney Burns?"

Danny studied Kevin's face in the moment it took for him to respond. He seemed irritated but fighting to appear calm.

"Why would you ask me that?"

"Angela told me. She said someone saw you kissing Britney."

"Listen, Danny, you're better off letting that bitch go. Stop talking to her. She's jealous of us and she'll say anything, even lie, to turn you against me. I shut her down at the séance, but I won't always do that. And I've heard things about her too."

"Like what?"

"Some people think she had something to do with Nancy getting messed up at the carnival."

Danny's blood chilled. Was Angela really capable of violence? Multiple times, even?

"Why would she do something so awful?" Danny pondered aloud.

"I don't know, but you better watch out for her. People are also telling me to stay away from you because you're her friend. They say you're both bad apples. Maybe I should be the one asking questions about lies and kissing other people."

Danny couldn't say for sure if he was a bad apple or not. "I'm sorry, Kevin."

"I guess you guys have been friends for a while and all, so must be difficult to hear bad about her. The truth hurts sometimes."

"I'm sorry. I shouldn't have asked you about this. You're probably right about Angela."

"Is this the reason you wanted to play twenty-one questions? Were you setting me up for this?"

"Yeah, I guess, but—"

"You should have just asked me about it, instead of playing games," scolded Kevin. "That was really... immature."

Danny realized he'd made a colossal mistake, and now Kevin was slipping away. No, no, no. He should have known better than to trust hearsay.

"Can you forgive me?" said Danny. He clutched Kevin's hand and placed it on his inner thigh. "Maybe I can make it up to you?"

Kevin stood up with a jolt. "I think you're right. We don't know each other that well. We should take this slower. Let's get to know each other better before we hang out like this again."

He gathered up his coat and bag, then turned to leave.

"Sorry, Danny."

2 2
BRITNEY'S BURN

*D*anny lingered at the water fountain after pretending to quench his thirst. He rummaged through his book bag, then flipped through a notebook, even though he had no reason to do these things. His empty actions went unnoticed within the commotion of Woodside High School's hallways during that morning's break.

He couldn't admit to himself why he was there, by that water fountain, across from her locker. Maybe he couldn't accept that Kevin had rejected him. Maybe his natural state was one of suspicion. Or was he more gullible and naïve?

Then he saw her.

The combination lock spun back and forth in her hands. She opened her locker.

She had dirty blonde hair styled high, piercing dark eyes, and sharp features, which she accentuated with her impeccable fashion. If she'd cared enough to try, she could have cakewalked a prom title, dated the star quarterback, or cultivated a gang of admiring devotees. Instead, she was a quiet loner who dated Rick Ward most of last year, the metalhead with long hair who cursed at a teacher and got expelled for smoking weed on school grounds.

Standing there at her locker, she seemed unfathomably cool and superior.

He must decide quickly: summon the courage to act now or let the opportunity pass and regret it.

Danny first met her in 6th grade when they shared the same class. Her demeanor was gruff even then, and she had become only more arrogant in high school. He suspected she would dismiss him or even humiliate him. Nevertheless, he left his station at the fountain and crossed the busy hallway over to Britney Burns.

"Uh, hi," squeaked Danny.

Britney paused for a glance at him, then continued sorting through books and papers in her open locker.

"Okay," she said, rolling her eyes.

"Have you seen Kevin lately?"

"I'm sorry, who the hell are you?"

"My name is Danny. We were in the same sixth grade class, remember? Anyway, I was just wondering if you've seen Kevin Pullman recently."

"What's it to you?"

"I...well, he..." Danny said, wiping his clammy hands on his jeans.

He should have planned this out ahead of time. Now he was dancing around the truth, playing games again. Manipulating. That didn't end well last time, so Danny steeled himself, and adopted a different strategy.

"Did you fuck Kevin?"

"Ha!" Britney squawked.

"I heard Kevin led you on and then dropped you."

"What's it to you? Oh, I get it. You heard I was a slut, and you want to shoot your shot? Not in this lifetime, barfbag. Piss off."

Undeterred, Danny explained, "I think he may have lied to me, too, about something very important. And I want to know the truth."

"Look, Kevin can take a long walk off a short pier. I don't give a shit about that jackass."

Britney slammed her locker shut, slung her bag over her shoulder, and faced him with crossed arms.

"Danny is your name? Yeah, I think he mentioned

you once. He said you're a queer. A nancy boy. Said you hit on him and he rejected you."

Britney fake-frowned at him. "Silly faggot, dicks are for chicks."

23

DREAM II

*D*anny returned from school in a daze. He made a beeline from the front door to his bedroom and dropped like a lead weight, face-first onto his bed. His red plaid comforter, freshly washed, smelled like detergent and dryer sheets—that soothing, fuzzy scent that seduced him to sleep every night.

Using his feet, he pried off one shoe, then the other, and pulled the edge of the comforter up and over his body, like a taco. He let the grainy, swirling colors behind his eyelids lull him to a soothing, deep sleep.

The night air was crisp. Fluffy flakes of snow drifted

down around him, coating everything with a thin layer of white.

He stepped up to the entrance gate of the carnival, noting the eerie blanket of quiet over what was usually a bustling din of activity. The cacophony of dings, swooshes and screams was gone, replaced by the ambient hiss of gentle wind gusts and the soft crunch of snow underfoot.

This isn't right, he thought. *Why is it snowing in October?*

Though the carnival rides inside were powered up, with their vibrant lights casting a blueish hue over the sparkling snow, none of them were operating.

At least that's how it seemed, until Danny noticed that the swing ride's seats were all splayed out in mid-air, as if they were spinning. Except they weren't. And the Super Loops ride, which swung in vertical circles, was suspended upside down.

As Danny stepped into the carnival, he realized that there were people everywhere, frozen in time, like statues. A family waiting in line at the ticket booth, a young girl stuffing purple cotton candy in her mouth, a full load of people seated in the Super Loops ride, with heads pointing down at the ground.

Danny advanced further inside the carnival and found himself among a motionless group of teens, all frozen with jovial expressions, as if someone had just cracked a joke.

He approached one of the laughing boys, whose face glittered with frost and whose eyes were fogged with white. Danny touched the boy's gray cheek with a pointed finger. Solid, like stone. He moved down to the collar of his denim jacket, gathering snowflakes. It crunched under the pressure of his finger.

Danny stepped past the teens and zigzagged his way through the crowds of ghostly people, toward the back of the carnival.

He paused near the Hall of Mirrors. There were no frozen people heading inside, nor even a ticket taker at the entrance.

The gaping mouth of the entryway flickered with movement and a cloud of darkness emerged, churning inside out and folding in upon itself. A shape gradually formed—something vaguely human.

"Danny," it breathed.

Terror gripped Danny when he realized this thing, this darkness, was aware of him.

He stumbled backward.

The darkness moved toward him, trails of smoky black billowing away as it advanced.

Danny spun on his heels to run, but the snow slipped underfoot. He dropped hard onto his side.

The silhouette hardened, with increasing clarity and detail, like a camera lens focusing on a subject.

Arms appeared, then legs, then it sprinted toward him.

He scrambled to his feet and took off in the opposite direction. He dodged frozen people, slipping clumsily in turns around them. When he reached the center of the carnival grounds, he glanced back.

It was gone.

There were only his own frenetic footprints in the snow. Danny turned in circles, searching for a dark figure against the gleaming snow, but saw nothing.

He waited in place, unsure of what to do, until the magnetic pull of that place overtook him again. Despite his terror, he drifted back, returning to the exact spot he'd run from.

"Danny! It is your own death that seduces you," it shrieked, charging at him once again from the entrance of the Hall of Mirrors.

Again, Danny turned to run, and crashed directly into a frozen child who had just dismounted from the Zipper ride. They both toppled over onto the ground.

He couldn't run now; the darkness was nearly upon him.

Danny lunged past another frozen young boy, threw himself into the Zipper car, and wrenched the cage shut.

The darkness slammed into the Zipper car, rattling the cage mesh and rocking the car on its axis.

"I've got something to say to you, Danny," the dark figure rasped from the other side of the cage.

Danny slid on the bench seat to the far side and covered his face with his hands.

"Go away, go away, go away," he mumbled in a low tone, over and over.

When the thing failed to say anything else, and Danny became aware of the cold again, and the extended silence, he opened his eyes.

It was no longer on the outside of the car…

"Hello, Danny."

…it was now sitting next to him, with eyes white and clouded like the frozen people, a stark contrast against the otherwise faceless, dark body.

Danny let loose a shrill, ear-splitting scream.

He pulled up on the lap bar and shoved at the door, but it was locked. He shook it and pounded on the metal mesh in front of him, but it was no use. Danny was stuck in the cage with this ghastly silhouette with eyes.

"You must stay away from here," it said.

Danny's screaming gave way to panicked sobbing— until he felt a hand on his leg. It was a real human hand, like his own.

The blackness had dissipated, and in its place was Tommy.

"Who are you?" Danny pleaded.

"You know who I am, silly."

Warm tears streamed down Danny's face. "Why are we here?"

"We're here because you want to be here. You think this is where I am, but I am anywhere you are."

"What?"

"It's true. You've been carrying me around with you for far too long. Let's do what you wanted all along, Danny. Let's go our own way, eh? It doesn't have to be forever. I will always come back to you—should you need me, for any reason at all."

"No, I…"

"Let us split. One become two again."

"I can't. I need you. Please."

"And Danny…"

"What?"

"Stay away from the Hall of Mirrors."

24

SHIT SHOW

Danny applied a few thin brush strokes to his *Teen Wolf* mask, then set it on the drying rack so he could clean up his work area.

Later that night was the first of several art openings Mrs. Donahue had scheduled for the school year, and this one was Halloween themed. She encouraged all her seniors to wear their masks for the event, so several others had popped into the art room after school to finish their projects. Danny wondered if Claudia would be one of them, but she wasn't.

As he wiped up his paint splatters and washed his brushes in the sink, his thoughts returned to the events of the previous day.

Britney's insults, his nap, the dream.

Danny had woken from his vivid dream to a wet pillow, soaked with tears. He giggled at the idea that he, too, was a bedwetter, in his own way.

His mood had shifted after the dream. A calm had come over him.

He and his mother had eaten TV dinners together while watching reruns of *Laverne & Shirley*. Danny shared nothing about his day with her. He'd passed the rest of the evening in a reflective mood. He sketched, listened to Nick Cave records, then blankly stared at the ceiling.

He wished someone would tell him what to do, how to end all the confusion and pain. By the end of the night, Danny was still undecided whether to go to the Hall of Mirrors, like Tommy—or Maggie—had urged him to do.

He wanted to believe that his dream was a premonition, that the warning from Tommy about the Hall of Mirrors was real. That would mean Angela was right about everything. But she had admitted to lying about very important things and could be lying about much more. Was she enraged enough by Tommy breaking up with her that she had left him in the treehouse drunk, knowing he would die?

Kevin, who encouraged him to go to the Hall of

Mirrors, was also a liar, if Britney was to be believed. Could Danny forgive him? Being honest with other people about their relationship was too risky. Britney's venom was proof of that. Maybe Kevin lied to protect himself, or both of them. Some would go even further than lying to protect themselves.

By the time Danny finished cleaning up, the art room was empty. He had just a couple of hours to grab dinner before the art event started at seven o'clock. He flicked the lights off and left.

A zombie, a vampire, and a black cat barreled through the darkness behind Danny. Moaning, hissing, and meowing, they scampered past him in their masks and continued up the walkway to enter Woodside High School's main door.

A pang of jealousy sliced through him. That could have been him, with Tommy or Kevin or Angela, or all of them. What a faraway dream that seemed to him now. He had no real friends anymore. No confidants, no companions. He was alone. Was that his own doing?

"Hello…? You going in or not?"

Lost in thought, Danny stood blocking the front door.

"Oh, I'm sorry," he said, and proceeded inside.

"You're behaving even weirder than usual," said

Claudia, following him in.

Danny was surprised to see her, and more surprised that she had said something to him. "Oh, well, I'm weird, I guess. Forgive me?"

"I need to touch base with Mrs. Donahue before the show starts," said Claudia, "but do you have a minute after that? To talk?"

"Oh yeah, uh, while you do that, I need to run to my locker and drop off my coat. Meet me at the top of the central staircase in a few?"

"See you then," Claudia said. She bounced up the stairs toward the art room on the second floor, looked over her shoulder, and added, "Nancy pulled through. She woke up from her coma."

At 6:40 p.m., the building was mostly deserted, except for his classmates cavorting in their masks. Some of them went further than just masks and dressed in full costumes from the neck down. Others, like the pumpkin-faced girl that just walked by, wore all black to focus attention on the hand-crafted mask. Danny figured he could get away with wearing his regular street clothes, since Teen Wolf was a high school student himself.

Nevertheless, he didn't need his coat.

Eager to hear what Claudia had to say about Nancy, he fumbled with his combination lock, had to start over twice, but eventually threw the door open.

Did Nancy remember what had happened to her?

Danny hooked his coat inside his locker and slammed the door shut.

Wait.

Something out of place had caught his eye.

He opened his locker again, and there, written in green marker on the mirror hanging on his locker door, was a new message.

Meet me in the Hall of Mirrors tomorrow
—Tommy

Danny flung around, looking for a culprit. Of course, no one was there. This must have been done earlier. But it wasn't there when Danny left school just a couple of hours ago. It was recent.

Danny checked the edges of the locker for any sign of forced entry. None.

Who could have accessed his locker? Someone with the combination? An administrator? A teacher who didn't like him? Dr. Hughes in guidance?

Angela.

Lockers were assigned freshman year and students retained them all four years. Tommy and Danny had both provided their lock combos to her in sophomore year when they were sick with the flu. She'd retrieved all of their books and notebooks for them. That was a long time ago, but no other student in school ever had Danny's locker combination.

Danny felt violated, just like when the pink panda appeared in his car.

Or was this a message from Tommy? Danny relaxed at the thought.

He ran his fingers over the message on the mirror, then looked past it, at himself.

A wail and then a heavy thud from down the hall.

Danny slammed his locker shut again and sprinted toward the awful sound, careening around a corner. Claudia was splayed at the bottom of the central staircase, her witch mask flung away from her motionless body.

Danny raced over and shook her shoulder. A trickle of blood spilled out of her hair.

"Claudia, Claudia!" he cried. "What happened? Are you okay?"

Her eyes opened, rolled back, and she groaned.

Danny looked around for help; there was no one nearby. He could hear the art students upstairs, but they were too far away.

Claudia groaned again and rubbed the side of her head, leaving a smear of blood on her hand.

"Ow…"

Her gaze wandered until it fixed on him, and her

pained face transformed into an expression of terror.

"Get away from me," she pleaded. "No, No! Get away from me!"

"What?"

"You creep! I knew it was you!"

"What do you mean?"

An elderly man and woman passed through the front door. Guests of the exhibition were arriving now.

"I don't know what game you're playing," cried Claudia, "but I saw your mask. I know it was you who pushed me down the stairs. I know the *Teen Wolf* mask is yours, Danny! Get the hell away from me!"

"What are you talking about? I don't have my mask."

"You hurt Nancy too. You creep!"

Claudia pulled herself up from the floor and wobbled before catching her balance.

"You will pay for this!" she warned, then disappeared out the front door of the building.

"Everything okay?" asked the elderly man.

Danny ascended the steps of the central staircase two at a time. He passed pumpkinhead, black cat, zombie, and vampire, and burst into the art room.

"Oh, hello Danny," said Mrs. Donahue.

"Where is it?"

"Hmm?"

"My mask, did you move it?"

"No, I haven't moved any masks. Did you misplace it?"

Danny's hands shook uncontrollably, his stomach turned over.

The drying rack was empty.

His mask was gone.

Danny paced in his living room.

What the hell was happening? Had he slipped into a dream? Life didn't feel real anymore. Was he losing his mind? Had he lost it a long time ago? Nothing made sense.

Danny tried weighing the pros and cons of telling his mother everything when she came home. Would she send him away to some loony bin? Maybe she'd be able to help him sort through the mess. But would she hate him if she knew what happened the night Tommy died? The more he thought, the more his brain flooded with anxiety, until he couldn't concentrate at all.

And where was his mother? She told him that morning that she had to stay late at work, but that she'd be home by eight o'clock. At 8:25 p.m., she still wasn't home. Where was she?

Calm down, he told himself, taking a deep breath.

He parked himself on the couch, placed his hands

on his knees, and tried to focus on his breathing.

Calm.

Inhale, exhale.

A vision of Claudia's bloody head invaded his mind. Poor Claudia.

And she thought it was Danny who'd pushed her down the stairs! By now she had likely told someone—a teacher, her parents, a police officer. Would they be coming for him soon? How would he defend himself against any accusations?

If Angela had been in the school building to leave that mirror message in his locker, she could have swiped the mask from the art room while she was there, then waited somewhere until she had an opportunity to push Claudia. But why would she hurt Claudia? They were the only two in the Hall of Mirrors with Nancy. Did Claudia witness something in there that would implicate Angela?

Maybe he should call Angela at home and confront her before more terrible things happened. What would Tommy do?

With a trembling hand, Danny picked up the phone from the end table.

What if it wasn't her, though? Danny would look like he'd lost his mind or even look desperate to blame someone else for something he did.

The dial tone droned at him, insisting he make up

his mind.

He had to know what she'd say…

He dialed the first three numbers of Angela's phone number, before a sound in the next room startled him.

The doorknob twisting in the front door.

Danny put the phone down and peeked around the corner in time to see his mother shuffle in; through the open door beyond her, he saw a police cruiser idling in the street.

His mother didn't look happy.

"I, I don't know what's happening," Danny said. "There must be something wrong and I—"

"It's okay," his mother interrupted, shutting the door. "The police officer drove me home. Some jerk ran me off the road, straight into a ditch. I couldn't get my car started again."

Danny breathed a sigh of relief. The cop wasn't there for him.

But someone had tried to hurt his mom. She was all he had left in this world.

"I was less than a mile from Aunt Jean's house," she said, peeling off her jacket, "so I just walked there. I called the police, though I don't know what they'll be able to do."

"Did you see the driver in the other car?"

"I couldn't see the other driver or even what kind of

car it was. But there is a police report now."

"Okay, okay, okay."

Danny was still shaking.

"Aww, honey, it's okay. I'm fine. And I'm home now. If I had known you were back from the art show already, I would have called from Aunt Jean's to let you know what was going on. Why are you home early?"

Danny couldn't find the words, so he didn't bother. He hugged her, then retreated to his room.

2 5

HALL OF MIRRORS

*I*t was Saturday, the last night of the carnival. Thankfully, there were no calls from the police or school administrators about Claudia. After deliberating all day, Danny had made his decision. He hadn't told his mother about anything. Instead, he would go to the Hall of Mirrors.

Someone, or something, made it clear last night that the danger surrounding him was accelerating. Danny didn't know if he could trust Tommy's messages, as they seemed to conflict. At the séance Tommy directed him to the Hall of Mirrors, but the Tommy of his dream told him not to go. But he didn't have time to think more about it; he could not be passive, he had to act. If that meant confronting someone, including his own darkness, in the Hall of Mirrors, then he must go.

Danny parked his car in Woodside Farm's mostly vacant lot.

Instead of heading into the carnival, he made a detour first. Many of the floodlights used to illuminate the perimeter of Woodside Farm were already shut off, including those above the corn maze. Danny crept across the lot in near darkness and slipped under the chain barrier at the exit of the maze.

He climbed a hay bale and stood facing the scarecrow. He gently tugged Tommy's purple flannel shirt off the scarecrow and tied it around his waist.

10:55 p.m.

Time to do this.

On his way inside, Danny passed a few stragglers leaving the fairgrounds. Most of the gaming booths were already closed, and none of the rides were operating. The place was deserted, much like in his dream. He shuddered on his way past the Zipper ride.

As he approached, Danny noticed that Madam Maggie's tent was gone, leaving a gaping hole on the perimeter of the carnival, exposing the woods beyond.

Next door, the Hall of Mirrors was abandoned by the ticket taker, but red and green lights pulsed from within. He paused at the entrance and listened. He could not hear any voices inside. Strangely, there was no stanchion blocking entry, as if the place were welcoming him.

He stepped in.

The short entry hall turned hard right and opened into a wide corridor with a few distorting mirrors—the kind he'd seen in a boardwalk funhouse. Danny wasn't sure what he was supposed to be looking for in this place, so he stopped at each one. The first one reflected long legs that reached up to his neck, the next was a compressed body with a large egg head, and finally, a mirror that made him appear wider than he was tall.

These mirrors have an agenda.

Mirrors lie, he thought.

Leaving the distorting mirrors behind, Danny climbed a short ramp and turned a sharp right into the main mirror maze. Strips of dim lights at his feet divided the floor in an endless pattern of inter-locking triangles. At the corner of each triangle rose a column, creating the effect of a forest of columns stretching into infinity before him.

The alternating red and green lights disorient-ed him as he inched forward, arms outstretched. It wasn't until he came within steps of a mirror ahead of him that his reflection appeared suddenly beside him and his hand crashed into the mirror. Once, twice. The dimness of the lights frustrated his sense of space.

Clank, click.

Danny swiveled in place at the sound of something heavy and metallic to his left. Was someone else in there with him now? Battling an instinct to run, he held firm, listened. Nothing else. Anyway, he didn't come in here to run away from things. He came here to confront something, to get answers.

Red, green, red, green.

Danny sensed an open path to his left and stepped in that direction, moving toward the sound.

Right, left, *crash.*

Danny wiped sweat off his forehead with the sleeve of Tommy's purple flannel.

He noticed a break in the pattern. One side of a floor triangle was missing and the space beyond shifted the infinite pattern at an odd angle. The mirror wall connected to it seemed to jut forward, like a door slightly ajar. Danny fingered the edge and pulled it, swinging the mirror forward, revealing a shallow vestibule leading to a large metal door.

Danny checked the back of the mirror to make sure it didn't have a locking mechanism that would engage behind him. Nope. He stepped forward into the passageway. As the mirror swung closed behind him, darkness engulfed the space except for a thin beam of faint bluish light leaking underneath the door ahead. He groped in the darkness for the handle of the large door in front of him, then, finding it, pushed open the door.

The woods.

He was looking through a backdoor, onto the wooded embankment behind the Hall of Mirrors. A rusted old metal staircase descended from the door, but the last step didn't touch the ground—it hung suspended a couple feet above the downward sloping terrain…

…where Nancy was found.

Danny shivered at the thought, backed away, and reentered the Hall of Mirrors.

Red, green, red, green.

He heard screeching and metallic thuds and crashes coming from outside as some of the carnival amusements were disassembled or folded up for transport. He remembered in past years when, after closing night, every trace of the carnival had disappeared before daybreak. How much time did he have before someone came to pack up the Hall of Mirrors?

Danny continued through the maze.

The dim colored lights flickered off, then returned a few seconds later.

He searched around to see if anything had changed. Endless triangles and columns, nothing out of place.

He caught his own gaze in the closest reflecting mirror and paused. *Is that you, Tommy? Am I Tommy?*

Red, green, red, green.

Purple, orange. Under the colored lights, he couldn't see the true colors of his flannel shirt—Tommy's flannel shirt—but he knew in his heart it was purple. Maybe he was wrong for wearing it, but he yearned to be near Tommy that night, to see him. Maybe it would provide some kind of talismanic power.

"Tommy, please," Danny cried, "if you are here, please say something. Give me a sign."

Where was he? Was Danny supposed to do something? Like say Bloody Mary or Beetlejuice three times?

"Tommy, Tommy, Tommy."

Danny slumped against the wall and let his weight drop to the floor, still gazing at his reflection. He touched his cheekbones, searched his own eyes.

The twins looked more like their father than their mother. But their father was never proud of Danny, never seemed to claim him as his own. So when Tommy died, he abandoned what was left of their family. Danny never would have done that. Though he looked like Dad, he did not ever want to be like him.

"Are you here, Tommy? I need you."

When Dad discovered that Tommy had been drinking that night, he totally flipped his wig, accused Danny of corrupting him. Danny was the free spirit, the risk taker, so it was easier to believe that he'd have alcohol. By all outward appearances, Tommy knew what he wanted in life, walked the straight and narrow, and succeeded at everything, but Danny was a floundering, artsy-fartsy enigma who painted his nails black sometimes and kept secrets.

"Why am I here?" Danny asked. "If you need my help, Tommy, please talk to me."

A voice responded.

"Sounds like maybe you're the one lost and in need of help, not Tommy," it said, chuckling.

Danny leapt up, spun in circles. He couldn't see anyone, but the voice had been close by.

"Hello? Who are you? Where are you?"

"Come and find out. I'm over here."

Danny moved in the direction of the voice. It was a male voice. Familiar.

"Where? Say it again. I can't see you."

"Over here, babe."

A chill went down Danny's spine.

He turned left and saw the body.

A bloody body.

Red, green, red, green.

A sweater soaked in blood. A middle-aged man on his back. Eyes open, blank stare directed at the ceiling.

Mr. O'Quinn's dead body.

What?!

And then Danny saw who was standing over the body.

Kevin Pullman.

"I'm sure you're even more confused than you were a few minutes ago."

Danny's mouth moved, but no words came out.

"He is a very terrible man," said Kevin. "No, *was* a terrible man—he's very *dead* now."

"Did you...kill him?"

"He had it coming."

"You didn't do this for me, did you?"

Danny panicked. Had Kevin's protectiveness gone off the rails?

Kevin laughed. "In a way, yes, I did. The cops are coming. Should be here any minute. When they get here, you'll be here, and I won't. Get it?"

"No, I don't."

"Well, what do you think they'll do when they find a deeply disturbed kid all alone with a dead body? A kid who has claimed responsibility for the death of his twin brother? A kid who's been nearby when bad things happen? A kid who has written a confession in his own sketchbook?"

"No. I didn't write that."

"It's in your own handwriting, babe."

"But… How…"

"Our little study session made you awfully tired, didn't it? Sorry about that. I had to make sure you were knocked out, so I could get my own personal studying done. You've got a lot of interesting things in your bedroom. A sketchbook… A pink panda… A locker combination…"

Danny calculated the meaning of Kevin's words.

"Did you break into my car?"

"I had to make you suspect, at least for a while, that you could be a murderer. In the end, it's what led you here, isn't it?"

"Why? Why would you do this to me?"

"O'Quinn needed to die. And I'm not too keen on going to prison, so…"

Now it made sense. The rage was never about protectiveness. Kevin had some other reason for hating Mr. O'Quinn.

"You're the one who hurt Nancy and Claudia? And my mom?!"

Danny's blood boiled. He took a step toward Kevin, who raised a pistol at him with a gloved hand. He really was trying to get away with murder.

"Watch it. You'd better stay where you are," warned

Kevin. "And for the record, I didn't hurt Nancy. The dumb bitch somehow found the back door of this place and fell out of it. Tumbled right into the woods. I saw it. We really didn't need that extra attention from the cops, and we almost called off our plan. In the end, we figured we'd try to use it to our advantage."

"Wait...*we?*"

"Madam Maggie and me."

"No."

"Definitely, yes."

"But the séance. It felt so real."

"That's because she's damned good at what she does. I should know—she's my mother."

The cruel truth struck Danny like an intruder, a violation of his most vulnerable self.

"Madam Maggie is...a fake?"

"The best there is. And with my help scouting and feeding her information, even better."

Something about Kevin's voice was different. Sharper, smarter.

"And you're a fake?"

"Runs in the family, I suppose."

If Kevin was a fake, so was their time together. Danny could not believe that. It had been so real to him. Or was it too good to be true? Were there signs he missed?

"Don't worry," said Kevin. "The place you're

headed will have plenty of desperate guys interested in a young man like you. When one door closes, another opens, as they say."

Police sirens wailed somewhere far away, getting louder.

"I'll tell the police," Danny threatened. "I'll tell them the truth."

"Won't do any good. You don't know the whole truth anyway, do you? Besides, you've got a history of mental illness, you've confessed to hurting people in the past, and you just failed a test in O'Quinn's class, which is a petty but plausible motive for someone as unstable as you. The police have already been informed about your erratic behavior here at the carnival tonight…breaking in after hours, screaming obscenities and waving a gun around."

"But I didn't—"

"And another thing you should know…the police chief owes us a favor. He's a fan of Madam Maggie's too."

No. Danny could not accept this. He lunged to his right and took off the way he'd come, until he mistook a mirror for an opening and crashed headfirst into a dark sleep.

26

CATCH & RELEASE

*T*hundering footsteps woke him. Bright white lights now, no more red and green. His finger felt stuck in something.

Danny pushed himself up from the floor. He was still in the Hall of Mirrors, next to Mr. O'Quinn's dead body again. He must have been dragged back. And he now held the pistol in his own hand, finger on the trigger.

"Drop the gun! Put your hands up!"

Danny complied with the officer's command. "Sir, I didn't hurt Mr. O'Quinn, I promise."

One of two officers grabbed his arm, spun him

around, and handcuffed him in a single quick movement. A uniformed carnival worker appeared to
guide them out of the Hall of Mirrors.

Danny searched the area outside as they emerged.
Kevin was not there. Several more officers joined
them as carnival workers gawked.

"Look, I can tell you what happened. I came here
to meet my dead brother's spirit, but Kevin, Kevin
Pullman, he—"

The officer cut him short with a strong jerk on his
arm.

*Oh my God, this is happening. Kevin's plan is
working.*

They headed toward the parking lot, where red and
blue lights from a group of police cruisers lit up the
area. There were over ten policemen there.

The first officer passed him off to another, who
shoved him into the backseat of a car. The door
slammed, and the world shrunk down to an eerie,
muffled silence.

Danny hung his head. It still hurt from running
into a mirror. Did he knock himself out?

So, he'd been conned—savagely deceived, for
reasons he did not understand. The little that Kevin
revealed to him only led to more questions. Most
importantly, why was Mr. O'Quinn dead?

He supposed it didn't matter. If Kevin and Maggie

had the police chief in their pocket, he was doomed.

A familiar voice just outside the car interrupted his hopeless spiral of thoughts.

Angela.

She was talking with the officer who had arrested him. She had a camera slung around her neck. A polaroid camera, just like Tommy's. And she had photos too.

What is she doing? Did she conspire with Kevin and Maggie? No, she'd been right about everything— sort of.

Angela looked agitated. She pointed at the carnival, then at the photos. The police officer signaled for others to come look at what she had. Upon seeing the photos, some of them took off running into the carnival.

The first officer returned to the cruiser and opened the door.

"Danny, I'm going to take these cuffs off you, then ask you some questions. Can you tell me what you were doing at the carnival tonight?"

When Danny had finished recounting the entire sequence of events, including a brief backstory about Tommy, the police officer thanked him and told him to sit tight.

"What is happening now? Why is Angela here? Why did she come to the carnival?"

"Why don't I let her explain?" the officer said, leaving the door open.

Moments later, Angela was climbing into the back of the cruiser with him.

"Scoot over, Daniel-san," she said, smiling. His animosity toward her evaporated. Tears welled in his eyes.

"What in the fuck happened? Ange, Mr. O'Quinn is dead."

"I know."

"I didn't kill him!"

"I know."

"What else do you know?"

"I know that Kevin and Madam Maggie killed him. I was there. And I have proof."

"The pictures?"

"Yep."

"Is that Tommy's camera?"

"Yes. I took it when I was at your house earlier this week. I snuck into your bedroom before I left, when I was supposed to be in the bathroom. I'm sorry."

"Why did you take it? How did you know you would need to use it?"

"You didn't believe me that Kevin was dating Britney. I wanted to prove that he wasn't who you thought he was, and a camera would help. I followed him all week. Did you know he works for the carnival?

He lives in a trailer with Madam Maggie."

"That's his mother," Danny explained.

"Ha!"

"Why did they kill O'Quinn?"

"That, I don't know. When I arrived tonight, they already had him tied up behind the Hall of Mirrors. He was drugged or something. I was hiding in the woods, back where they found Nancy. I took a picture of them when O'Quinn was still alive because it was so bizarre. What they were doing looked suspicious. Then Kevin shot him. Like nothing. As casual as a handshake or a sneeze."

"Right there? Behind the Hall of Mirrors?"

"Yes. The carnival had ended by then, and they were breaking down the rides. Lots of banging and stuff, so that must be why no one heard it, or thought anything of it. Cunning bastards."

Danny remembered the open door at the back of the Hall of Mirrors. Kevin must have forgotten to secure it after dragging O'Quinn inside.

"Did they use the back stairs to drag him into the Hall of Mirrors?"

"Yes. I was able to get a couple of pictures when they were lifting him up there."

"Oh my God, I was already in there when they killed him. I heard banging but didn't realize it was a gunshot."

"The police know what happened. They believe me, but still, they found you with a dead body, so they might not release you tonight."

"Kevin said the police chief is on their side and will lie for them. I'm doomed."

"They have irrefutable photo evidence. And I kept some photos as insurance. Don't worry, they will determine that you were a victim too."

"Do they know where Kevin and Maggie are now?"

"Madam Maggie's tent was packed up early tonight, most definitely to make a quick getaway. They aren't here, but they can't be too far."

"Ange, thank you."

"I told you I wasn't gonna give up on you. In fact, I made a promise to look out for you."

"Huh?"

"Danny," said Angela, making her voice smaller. "Your brother knew that you are gay."

The word thundered through him like a freight train.

Gay.

It hung in the air, like snot dripping out of a nose—embarrassing, disgusting to many, but perfectly human. Gay. It had been spoken, and Danny was stunned.

"What?"

"Tommy knew about you," Angela reiterated. "He

was worried. He could see you withdrawing, becoming antisocial. People can be cruel and narrow-minded, and he knew that. He wanted to protect you, that's all. He always had your well-being in mind. That's why our relationship was a secret, and why we broke up. He didn't want you to ever feel like a third wheel with us, or feel you were losing me as a friend. He didn't want to hurt you."

For the first time since Tommy died, Angela and Danny wept together.

"I love you, Danny. And your brother loved you, so much. He couldn't bear to be separated from you in college, not because he wanted to get in your way or because he was codependent, but because he wanted to make sure you were okay. He made me promise that night that I would always look out for you, too. So that's what I did, and what I'm doing now."

Danny took Angela in his arms and squeezed her.

"I'm so sorry I ever doubted you, Ange. My guardian Angel-a."

She pulled away from him, laughing through tears.

"Okay, that was corny as hell."

Danny laughed, and it was like old times.

But when that euphoric feeling faded, he realized that the answer to one of his burning questions might be within grasp, after all.

"Angela, how was Tommy when you left him that

night? I mean, was he still angry? Do you think he forgives me?"

"Danny, you know the answer to that question already."

"Huh?"

"Of course he forgives you. That's who he was—he never stayed angry for too long, never held a grudge. I've already told you that when I left Tommy in the treehouse that night, he was ready to head home and talk to you. He was over it."

"Why didn't he come home then?"

Angela grabbed Danny's chin and pulled his face up to meet hers.

"I don't know, and it doesn't matter. You are not responsible for his death. You had a fight, a down-and-dirty fight, like a lot of siblings have. His death was an accident. A terrible accident, and that's all."

Danny believed her.

He didn't need Tommy's spirit to tell him anything.

He believed her.

EPILOGUE

"*T*he police apprehended them just a few miles away," said Danny. "The huge, colorful trailer was too conspicuous. You think they would've ditched it, but I suppose they really thought they'd get away with murder."

"Do you know why Kane enrolled in Woodside High School?" asked Dr. Hughes.

That was Kevin's real name. Kane Paulson.

Danny was back in the guidance office, with the same fake plant, but a different attitude this time.

"I don't know for sure, but my guess is that he wanted to get as close to Mr. O'Quinn as possible. They thought he'd be easier to manipulate if Kane was his student. Keep your enemies close, as they say."

"Danny, you've probably heard by now what motivated the Paulson family to murder, but I've had a look at our records and reviewed some of the historical reporting. I have some answers. Nothing is confidential, so I'd be happy to share what I uncovered. I've spoken to the police about it."

"Well, I have heard some things, but I'm interested in hearing what you know."

"Of course. So, Scott O'Quinn was a teacher here at Woodside for twenty-five years, and his father was a district administrator. One of his students, Linda Paulson, filed several complaints against Scott for sexual harassment."

"Is that Kane's sister?" Danny speculated. If so, he already knew how this would end.

"Yes. The Paulson family was living here in Woodside in the seventies, before they became carnies. Well, nothing came of the complaints filed against Scott, probably because of his father's powerful position in the district. Linda was distraught over the lack of justice and took her own life. The Paulsons then started a campaign of harassment against the O'Quinns. They told the *Woodside Journal* that Scott was responsible for Linda's fragile emotional state and for her suicide. When Mr. Paulson, the father, died unexpectedly, Maggie and Kane left town. They've harbored this resentment for ten years, it seems."

"Wow."

So Kane was honest about some things. His sister really did commit suicide when he was just a kid. Telling Danny about her was a liability. Why would he do that if he was trying to get away with a heinous crime?

"Our records here show that Linda had many problems, not just with Mr. O'Quinn. She was a deeply disturbed girl who had her own rap sheet, which may have been why Scott targeted her. These creeps always look to exploit the vulnerable."

"That's sad. An obviously screwed-up family. Well, two screwed-up families, doing screwed-up things," Danny added.

"How are you handling all this now, kiddo? It's been about a month since…"

Danny looked down and picked at the cuticle on his left thumb, flaking off some of the newly applied black polish.

"I am adjusting…to reality. I am seeing a therapist now. My mom and Angela are super supportive now that…that everything's out in the open. My application to the School of Visual Arts in New York is just about ready. I'm hopeful about the future."

"Excellent, Danny. What a pleasure to hear."

Danny had accepted that there was no darkness

within him after all, only a weakness, exploited by other people with both weakness and darkness inside them. Danny made a vow to never let that happen again.

"You know, Dr. Hughes, I wouldn't wish this on anyone, but for me, it helped. It was what I needed, as ironic as that may sound."

"I don't think anyone needs to get caught up in a murder, but I understand what you mean."

She opened her desk drawer and withdrew an envelope. "It was an honor to write your letter of recommendation."

"Thank you, Dr. Hughes. It means a lot to me."

"You are very welcome. Anytime you want to chat, stop in and say hello!"

"Before I go," said Danny, fumbling with a brown paper grocery bag at his feet, "I wanted to give you a gift, a token of my appreciation."

He withdrew a small, bushy green plant from the brown bag and placed it on Dr. Hughes' desk.

"It's a peace lily."

"Oh my! Danny...that's beautiful!"

She pulled it close and stroked the single white bloom poking out of the foliage.

"The nursery said it's a great office plant. It only needs to be watered once a week and thrives in low light."

"It's just lovely. Thank you so much."

"Dr. Hughes, I'm wondering…can I take this off your hands now?"

Danny picked up the fake plant on the edge of her desk and blew dust off the faded green plastic leaves.

Dr. Hughes chuckled. "Of course."

Danny left Dr. Hughes' office and rejoined his friends in the hall.

"Did you get it?" asked Claudia.

Danny held up the envelope, smiling.

"Well, let's go then!" said Nancy. "I'm ready for some ice cream!"

"Daniel-san," said Angela, looking ornery. "Can I get pink jimmies on my ice cream cone and still be the badass goth chick of your dreams?"

"Of course you can. Just don't listen to Morrissey!"

Angela threw her head back, laughing. "Never!"

Nancy skipped ahead of them, chanting "I scream for ice cream!"

Claudia shook her head. "Don't ask me how I know this, but I'm going to marry that crazy-ass bitch someday."

Hearing those words so freely spoken made Danny tingle all over with joy. Never in his life had he experienced such a sense of belonging. In that moment, he knew for certain he wasn't alone anymore. With friends like this, he could never be.

As the group filed out of the tall front door of Woodside High School, Danny made a pit stop at the nearby trash bin. He paused for a final glance at it, then tossed Dr. Hughes' fake plant through the flip lid, and it disappeared into darkness.

THE END

ACKNOWLEDGEMENTS

Mom and Jeff—thanks for sticking by me always, despite my mercurial nature. You are my foundation and my rock. Everything is possible because of you.

Special thanks to my editors, Peter Senftleben and Lauren Humphries-Brooks, for encouraging me to reach further, for making my book better than it was before your feedback, and for giving me the confidence to publish.

To Dustin Holden, and the rest of the amazing Instagram community I have experienced over the past year: thank you so much for your interest in my book and the support you've shown for a total newb!

And my dudes, R.L. Stine and Christopher Pike... Geez, thanks for the amazing summer of 1992, spent in my grandfather's hammock, reading tons of your books, one after the other. My book positively would not have been written without your inspiration.

ABOUT THE AUTHOR

Charles Ashe is a designer and visual artist. This is his first book. He lives in Delaware with his husband and their son Dorian (a grey tabby cat). When not writing, he enjoys oil painting, turning old typefaces into fonts, visiting museums, watching Britcoms, eating Indian food, and listening to retrowave music.

You can find him at
WWW.CHARLESASHE.COM

and on Instagram at
@CHARLESASHEBOOKS

Lightning Source UK Ltd.
Milton Keynes UK
UKHW021846090223
416682UK00014B/1712

9 781955 741149